# The Declaration

*Tales from a Revolution: South-Carolina*

# The Declaration

Lars D. H. Hedbor

*Brief Candle*
Press

Cover and book design: Brief Candle Press
Cover image based on "Sunrise over Forest and Grove," Albert Bierstadt.
Maps courtesy of Library of Congress,
  Geography and Map Division.
Fonts: Allegheney, Doves Type and IM FELL English.

First Brief Candle Press edition published 2014
www.briefcandlepress.com

ISBN: 978-0-9894410-6-3

# Dedication

*To the many friends*
*who carried me to this point*

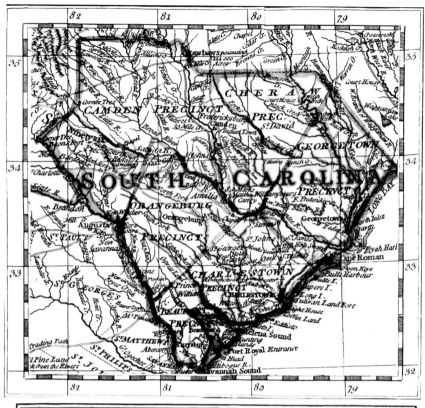

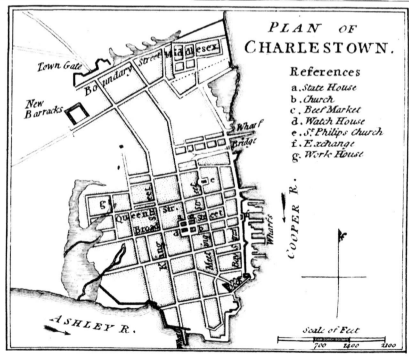

PLAN OF CHARLESTOWN.

References

a. State House
b. Church
c. Beef Market
d. Watch House
e. S.t Philips Church
f. Exchange
g. Work House

# Chapter I

As Katie pulled up to her Gram's familiar house and opened her car door, the smell of the autumn leaves in the crisp air transported her back to autumn visits in her childhood. Her joy at the welcoming air was tempered, though, by the knowledge that this was the last time she would come to her grandmother's home in the fall.

"Come in, child! How is my little Katydid?" Gram sounded the same as ever as she opened the door, but there was a new frailty in her movements, and the skin around her eyes seemed to be darker and more sunken than Katie could remember ever having seen it before.

"I'm doing fine, Gram. How are you feeling?" Katie entered the immaculate home and followed Gram into the kitchen, where the coffee was ready and cookies laid out, as always.

"Oh, well, you know, the scars from the last surgery are healing up well enough, and I'm back out of the chair, so that's all to the good." Gram cast a quick frown in the direction of folded wheelchair in the corner of the kitchen. "Have a cookie, child, and pour us some coffee, would you, dear?"

Watching her grandmother lower herself slowly, but with determination on her face, into the kitchen chair, Katie felt a surge of compassion for her. She wondered, for the thousandth time, whether they were doing the right thing in helping Gram into what was euphemistically called "assisted living." "Deathwatch warehouse" seemed more like it in Katie's jaundiced view.

They chatted over the cookies and coffee about inconsequential things: Katie's studies, her lack of a boyfriend, her latest knitting project. Finally, the conversation circled around to the real matter at hand. "Gram, where should I start on the packing?"

"Well, I always worked on any large cleaning project from the top to the bottom, so you had best start with the attic, I suppose. The good Lord only knows what all is stashed up there. You know your grandfather—he was the worst packrat you ever did meet. Always claimed that everything he kept would have some value, some deep meaning someday."

She chuckled. "Perhaps he's right, but I haven't been up there since he left us, and not much before then, so I really don't know what you'll find." She closed her eyes, a peaceful smile on her face, and spoke quietly, almost to herself. "Oh, Charles, you would be so proud to see your little Katydid, all grown up."

"Now, Gram, I'm hardly all grown up."

"Perhaps not quite, but, 'Well begun is half done,' right?" A cheerful sparkle shown in Gram's eye as she looked at her granddaughter.

"I suppose I'm doing well enough so far, Gram. And thanks."

"Merely stating the truth, my dear girl. Now, boxes are in the garage, and the Dumpster will be here tomorrow, so just bag up what will need to go in there for now, all right?"

Katie stood, bringing her cup and saucer to the sink automatically. "Okay, Gram. You're right, we don't really have any time to waste." She sighed and went out to the garage to collect a couple of boxes. She carried them upstairs, passing the guest room where she had spent so many happy summers. The same posters from Gram's trip back to Germany were still there, all umlauts and springtime flowers, though they were faded now from decades in the afternoon sunlight that streamed through the dormer window.

Katie ducked into the hallway where the attic stairs were located. She had been up there a few times as a child, and remembered it primarily as dusty and poorly lit, with the smell of ancient planking and aging mothballs heavy in the air. She recalled neatly stacked crates and boxes, and even a couple of what Katie had been morally certain were treasure chests in the far corner of the space.

She opened the door at the back of the hallway and slowly made her way up the steps, reaching for the pull string that would light the single bulb over the opening. Very little had changed since she'd last been up here, she noted as she reached the top of the ladder. Okay, so she did have to crouch to walk, where she once had been able to stand upright.

The boxes were still mostly intact, though, and the crates and chests she remembered seeing were still there, although coated in a thick layer of dust. In one corner of the attic, squirrels had clearly made a nest, partially shredding a stack of old newspapers. Katie could see a grim-faced Nixon peering up at her from one of the scattered and jaggedly cut bits of newsprint, and a few words of a headline about the latest action in Indochina.

Some of the boxes had started to sag with age, and one was leaning perilously, nearly ready to spill its contents across the rough pine planking laid over the ceiling joists. Katie's eye, though, was drawn to the old chests under the tiny window at the end of the room. Still hunched over, she approached them and knelt in front of the first, examining it. It was larger than she had remembered, but then she had never come this close to it as a girl. Sturdily built, standing on short legs with a heavy wooden lid and a hasp—with no lock in it, thankfully—the old chest looked to be built for the ages.

She slowly brushed the dust away from the tarnished plate mounted on its lid. It fell in soft clumps to the planks, raising a cloud of dust. After she sneezed once, then twice, which blew yet more dust into the air, Katie was able to bend close to the plate and look at it. Inscribed in a light, almost fanciful script was the name *Elizabeth Harris*, and *1768*. A thrill ran down Katie's spine as she realized that this chest—or at the very least, the plate on it—had been around since before the American Revolution.

She thought she recalled from her mother's genealogical research that Elizabeth Harris was an ancestor, so it was possible that this very chest had been in the family for almost two and a half centuries.

Katie was hesitant to disturb the relic further, but her curiosity got the better of her, and she found herself raising the hasp and then grunting with the effort of lifting the massive lid. Made of a single oaken plank, with hinges stiffened with age, it creaked upward until it rested against the wall behind the chest.

A miasma of naphtha rose out of the old chest, and Katie could see the shriveled cores of a dozen mothballs lying among the folds of the blanket that lay over the other contents of the chest. Gingerly, she moved the blanket aside, eager to know what lay beneath it.

To one side of the chest, there was a stack of more blankets, neatly folded and reeking of mothballs. In the center, there was a small wooden crate, which had some dark clothing folded within it, what looked like a pair of trousers on top, and a bit of lace sleeve visible beneath that.

To the other side of the chest, there was a thick stack of papers, bound in a satchel of dark brown cardboard or leather with faded red string. As Katie reached in and picked it up, the string crumbled and fell away. She gasped, but nothing fell from the satchel, and she carefully turned and placed the whole stack on top of a box beside her.

Opening the satchel slowly, she found a short document written in a hand that was quite difficult to decipher, but which had a row of red wax seals affixed to it along the left edge. Straining to read it, Katie could make out what appeared to be some sort of property deed, describing a block of land, which was roughly sketched out at the top of the page.

Moving very slowly and deliberately, Katie lifted the sheet of paper by its edges and set it aside, so that she could see the next page in the stack. This one seemed to be a letter, and the handwriting was somewhat easier to make out, lacking the flourishes and decorations that the first document had featured.

When she saw the date at the top, she gasped again. The document she was looking at appeared to have been penned in 1775, only a few short years after Elizabeth Harris had received this very chest. What she could read of it seemed to concern a request for certain household supplies, but she could make out neither the sender's name nor the recipient's.

Her hands shaking now, Katie carefully replaced the deed

and closed the folder. She now saw that another satchel of similar appearance had been beneath this one, but she wanted to consult with Gram before looking any further at the amazing contents of the old chest.

Walking slowly and cautiously, guarding the folder with her arms hugged to her body, Katie turned and made her way back to the ladder. When she arrived back in the kitchen, where Gram stood at the stove stirring something, she sat down and gingerly laid the folder on the table before her.

"What's the matter, child?" Gram asked, when she saw Katie's ashen face.

"I started with one of those old chests, Gram... do you have any idea what Grandpa kept in those?"

"No, we never really discussed it, Katie. If you're talking about the big blanket chests, I don't know if he ever even dug into those. His own grandfather probably put them up there." She chuckled. "Packrats, the whole lot of them. Grandpa came by it honestly. So, what have you found, then?"

"Well, I didn't want to handle these any more than I already have, and I think we need to get in touch with someone who knows how to handle old documents before we do much more with them. The first date I saw was 1775, Gram."

"Well, gracious! That must have been up there ever since your great-great grandpa dragged that chest into the attic. Let me think—I may know someone who can help us out. Your grandfather once had this young fellow working for him, but he went back to the University as a researcher. Fetch me the white pages, would you, please?"

Katie brought her grandmother the phone and the directory,

and the older woman thoughtfully paged through it until she found the name she wanted, and then dialed.

"George Branton? Hello, this is Helen Harris, you may recall my husband, Charles Harris?" She paused. "Oh, why thank you for saying so. Yes, it was quite a shock, but he always said that he'd go out with a bang rather than a whimper, didn't he? Well, listen, the reason I'm calling is that my granddaughter Katie—you remember Charles talking about her? Well, she's found some letters and things that I thought you might be interested in taking a look at."

Katie could hear the man's voice, muffled but discernible. "Oh? What sort of letters?"

"Well, we haven't really looked at them yet—she put them down when she saw that one of them had a date of 1775 on it, and we thought it best to leave them for an expert to handle."

Branton's voice seemed louder and clearer now to Katie. "*Seventeen* seventy-five, did you say?"

"Yes, that's what she saw on it."

"Gram, you know, the light up there..." Her grandmother shushed Katie with a finger to her mouth, listening to Branton.

"Well, if you're free this evening, you could come by after dinner... Okay, very good, we'll look forward to seeing you then. Thank you very much, George. Please say hello to your lovely wife for me, won't you? Okay, good-bye."

"So he's coming by this evening, then?"

"Yes, around seven, he said. Can't break away before then, but that's okay. Oh, dear, can you go stir that soup before it scorches? Cream of broccoli, your favorite."

Katie sighed inwardly and got up to attend to the stove.

She'd never had the heart to tell Gram just how much she detested broccoli, and she had actually developed a grudging taste for the rich soup over the course of so many summers.

"A bit more pepper, maybe, do you think, dear?" Katie tasted the soup. As usual, Gram was exactly right. A dash of pepper and a quick stir, and Katie declared it perfect. She reached into the cupboard for two soup bowls—the old ones with the blue fluting around the rims—and ladled the steaming soup into each.

She continued the routine of setting the kitchen table for lunch, her mind racing as she went through the well-established motions, dropping ice cubes into glasses, pouring tea from the ever-present jug in the refrigerator, pulling spoons from the silverware chest and napkins from their drawer. She wondered what they would find in the cache of documents, and whether her grandfather would finally be vindicated in thinking that his treasures would turn out to have real value.

Sitting across from Gram, she bowed her head and waited while her grandmother recited the blessing, familiar from a thousand summer meals at this table. "*Komm, Herr Jesu, sei unser Gast Und segne, was Du uns bescheret hast.*" The two women said "Amen" in unison, and both then reached for their napkins, unfolding them according to their well-graven ritual.

As had been their habit for years, neither said anything until after the first sip of soup and a quick gulp of iced tea. "There's not much chance that those papers aren't real, is there, Gram?"

"No, dear, I can't think of any reason for your grandfather—or his grandfather, for that matter—to have wanted fake things lying around." She pursed her lips, a distant, thoughtful look in her eyes. "I imagine that Grandpa is feeling pretty smug right now." She chuckled and returned her attention to her meal.

"I just can't believe that all of that stuff was just upstairs all of these years, and nobody happened to go through that chest until now." Katie shook her head and sipped at her iced tea.

"It is a wonder that none of you kids who played up there ever got into that chest," Gram replied. "I imagine that today wasn't your first time in the attic?" Her eyes twinkled with amusement as Katie blushed slightly.

"Well, I know that Grandpa always said to stay out of there, but, yes, I did go up and look around once or twice. But I never got into anything," she hurried to add.

"Well, I think you probably would have done less damage than the squirrels I heard running around up there last fall," Gram smiled.

"Oh, yes, I wanted to ask you about that. It looks as though all they got into was a stack of old newspapers. Nothing terribly important-looking, but maybe forty or fifty years old. I'll take a trash bag up with me after lunch for those."

"Certainly, yes, Katie. I know Grandpa set papers aside on the day that your Dad was born, as well as your aunt and uncles, but I doubt that any of them are any good now."

"No, they looked pretty well torn up," Katie replied. Her eyes fell upon the old satchel again. She felt an unexpected eagerness for the afternoon to pass, so that Grandpa's old friend could look at the papers within and give them some context. A shiver of anticipation ran down her spine as she wondered what history lay within the old bag.

# Chapter 2

Noting the color of the leaves, Justin Harris whispered reassurance to his horse as the young mare picked her way down a rocky slope. It certainly was a gorgeous autumn day, and he was eager to return to his home and family. As he began to see familiar landmarks along the road, he felt the natural tension between his shoulders start to relax.

The Cherokee had been relatively peaceful for the past few years, but the French had certainly been stirring up trouble all up and down the seaboard, supplying arms and rum to the Indians in an effort to disrupt trade and settlement in the English Colonies. Any time he traveled beyond the settled region around his home, Justin felt that old tension between his shoulder blades build up, as though expecting the sharpened head of an arrow to bite in at any moment.

Now, though, with the late afternoon sun slanting through the trees and the trilling of the songbirds he knew so well ringing in his ears, he could relax. As he came to the bottom of the hardscrabble slope, he could see the fresh marks of other travelers on this road. Horse droppings that looked to be from only this morning made him wonder who was traveling ahead of him, and regret that he had not met his fellow traveler on the road.

Some company other than the mare would have been a welcome break from the monotony and tension of riding from

Charles Town. It was only three days' riding, four in foul weather, but one was safer in a group. With the smell of fresh-fallen leaves warm in his nostrils, though, Justin could not hold on to his regret for long. He always relished the anticipation of the last few miles to home, and was, upon reflection, just as glad to enjoy them in solitude.

He wondered how the children were faring as malarial months set in. Every fall was a new terror for his young wife, as she worried over each shiver that the children suffered. Though their farm was somewhat up out of the bottom land where the fevers often seemed to reside, in a bad year, the pestilential fever would sweep out over the land, touching nearly every home from Charles Town to the Upcountry.

While his small farm could not yet justify a slave to help, Justin hoped to be able to afford the investment within only a few more years. The land was rich and fertile, and he was glad that the small field of tobacco he'd harvested last month had been so productive. It was a lot of work to take on without help, but the oldest boy would be big enough to at least guide the turkeys through the fields next summer, where they would feast on pests in the leaves.

His cousin outside of Charles Town had hinted at the possibility of the loan of a buck negro, but Justin had demurred for the time being, unwilling to be beholden to his wealthy relations so soon after breaking off to establish his own fortune. Jeremiah had called the slave in from the fields for Justin's inspection.

"He's a fine, strong one, that Terrance," Jeremiah had said, laughter in his voice, and his hands lying across his expansive belly. "Turn 'round for my cousin Justin, Terrance," he called out to the young man, whose skin was as black as night.

"Bred that boy right here on the plantation, Justin. His mam was just off the boat from Guinea, but his pap is an old fellow who's worked for Harrises near his whole life. Mam didn't make it through the fevers a few years ago, but Terrance here, he didn't mind leaving the house when he got big enough for the fields. Didn't care for my silly wife prayin' over him all the time."

Jeremiah raised his voice to call out to the black man. "That'll be all, Terrance. Now get back to the fields—you're behind on your work now." He gave a hearty laugh and dug Justin in the ribs. "Gotta keep them negroes hopping, you know? Doesn't do to have a blackbird sitting around, tryin' to think up ways to get themselves into trouble." Terrance silently turned and walked back to the fields, his stride long, but merely efficient, not overtly prideful.

Justin's eyes narrowed in thought as he rode. Terrance did not strike him as being one to worry about, unlike some negroes he'd seen. Slaves birthed and raised on the plantation rarely were, even if their dams were fresh from Africa.

Pondering it, he could see how having Terrance on the farm could make it possible to plant a more ambitious tobacco crop the next spring. He'd have to get some more land cleared, of course, but that could keep even a strong young buck busy for months. He decided that he'd ask Elizabeth whether she was comfortable with a negro on the farm, and if she agreed, he'd swallow his pride and write to Jeremiah.

After all, if the point of establishing his own homestead was to reach the point of being independent of the Charles Town Harrises' wealth, how better to achieve that than by bringing in a bigger tobacco crop next fall? Of course, making the shift from indigo planting to tobacco would be challenging for the negro, but nothing that an occasional touch of the whip couldn't help with.

He caught the first whiff of fragrant smoke from the cooking fire from his neighbor's place and sat up straighter on his mare. Digging his heels in slightly, he urged her to speed up a bit, but she needed no encouragement. Her own eagerness to return to the comfort of her familiar paddock was incentive enough for her to pick up her feet and walk more smartly.

Rounding the corner on the road as it wrapped around the hill behind his farm, he could see his simple home. One day, he hoped, he'd give Elizabeth a proper plantation home, but for the moment, she didn't seem to mind it, and the children were happy. As he rode down the slope to the house, Timothy spotted him and started running, shouting, "Papa! Papa!"

Elizabeth, hearing his excitement, emerged from the house, her face shining with her exertions in the kitchen. Justin rode up to her and swung out of his saddle, taking her into his arms for a long embrace. His son threw himself onto one of Justin's legs and wrapped his arms around it tightly, beside himself at the joy of seeing his father again. His baby daughter came to the doorway, where she solemnly regarded him, thumb stuck into her mouth. Her enormous dark eyes were like pools of ink, and after a moment, she turned and toddled back into the house.

"I am so glad to see you, Justin," Elizabeth murmured into his shoulder. "Old Thomas did come by every day, as you asked him to, and made sure that everything was taken care of around the farm, but I worry whenever you're traveling."

"I know, Elizabeth. It's pretty safe these days, though.

And I'm glad I went. Jeremiah's really becoming quite the figure in Charles Town. He also had an interesting offer for me." Justin outlined his thoughts on bringing Terrance to the farm, pointing out the advantages of being able to expand their tobacco crop sooner than he'd expected.

"I won't do it, though, if you don't like the idea of a negro on the farm, Elizabeth."

She considered for a moment and then said, "No, I don't think it will trouble me. I worry about what the children will make of it, but I know it's important for us to be able to improve our situation here."

Justin embraced his wife again. "The children will take it in their stride, once the novelty of the thing wears off. I'll write to Jeremiah and work out the details." He whirled around, looking at the land around his home. "I think we'll clear that section over there for the planting, and that area past there for the growing season."

He turned back to his wife, gesturing at the fields. "I'll be right inside. I am famished from the ride, but I want to check on the tobacco before I come in, all right?"

"Certainly, dearest. I have a good chicken stew started, and I just need to make some biscuits. It should all be ready before sundown."

He kissed her on the side of her head. "That sounds wonderful, dear. I won't be long."

Stretching his legs as he walked, Justin strode to the small structure where the tobacco hung, drying. The rich scent of the leaves, now faded from brilliant green to a deep tawny shade, filled his whole head with its heady odor—and the thought of the earnings they would bring. He'd have to hitch up the wagon and bring them in to the government house in just a few more weeks.

The soft weight of the leaves rustled slightly as he ran his hands over them gently. It had been a good crop, with nearly perfect weather, particularly at harvest time. A long summer of careful attention had yielded nearly as perfect a result as he could have hoped for.

He reflected that he might even be able to triple his crop next year, if Terrance were industrious enough. He'd have to get a letter off to his cousin with the next post rider, though, if he were to have enough time to clear the land.

Turning to look back out over the hollow where his house nestled, Justin sighed contentedly. Everything was going to work out well, he just knew it.

# Chapter 3

The afternoon's packing and clearing in the attic was uneventful, other than when Katie discovered the desiccated corpse of a squirrel in the pile of chewed newspaper. Generally an unflappable young woman, she was still a bit squeamish as she scooped up the creature's remains with some folded newspaper, and glad to be done with that part of the job.

She had made good progress identifying the contents of the boxes and deciding what to keep, what to put in the living room for the yard sale, and what to just huck into the Dumpster. A few minor treasures did show up—what appeared to be substantially complete collection of *LIFE* magazine from 1959 to 1972 accounted for several neatly labeled boxes and would probably fetch a tidy sum on eBay, Katie thought.

Other boxes were filled with what could only, charitably, be called junk. No fewer than four boxes, each labeled, enigmatically, "Kitchen Drawer," had appeared so far, and each seemed to be the cleared-out contents of the kitchen junk drawer. Loose toothpicks, crumbling rubber bands, doubled-up postcards, ketchup packets (some of which had met toothpicks in the boxes, with predictable—and unfortunate—results), dead batteries, half-used seed packets, candle ends, bent scissors... Katie began to understand how Gram could have felt at least a tiny bit justified in calling Grandpa a packrat.

One box contained nothing but mismatched socks, a whole box of them, musty in the absence of mothballs. Katie satisfied herself that they were not serving as cushioning for some greater treasure, and then brought them downstairs to sit beside the garage where the Dumpster would be placed tomorrow morning.

She was thankful for the broad, sturdy stairs. Of course, the house had been built before the introduction of the rickety pull-down style of attic access favored in more recent construction—although, she realized, these stairs had also encouraged all too much easy storage of box after box of detritus.

Her eyes strayed to the old blanket chest frequently as she worked, having consciously started at the far end of the attic from where it sat beside its smaller companion. She knew that she would eventually feel compelled to at least open the other one, but she was saving that as a minor reward to herself for reaching the halfway point in her progress across the attic.

She pulled yet another wooden crate towards her, being careful not to give herself splinters on its rough-hewn boards. A quick glance revealed a stack of mixed magazines dating from the late 1970s and early 1980s. Reagan's cheery grin faced some dour-looking fellow over the headline "Yet Another Soviet Leader." Katie quickly flipped through the rest of the stack—who in their right mind would keep TV Guides, anyway?—and stooped to carry it down to the Dumpster pile.

As she walked down the stairs into the coolness of the house, Katie realized just how hot it was up in the attic. She dropped the crate on the gravel beside the garage and ducked back into the kitchen for some iced tea. Gram sat in her recliner in the next room, working on a crossword puzzle. Katie joined her, sitting on the couch and wiping beads of sweat from her forehead.

"How is it coming along, Katie?"

"Oh, I'm making good progress. You're right—there hasn't been a whole lot else up there to justify Grandpa's habit of keeping *everything*. Did you know about the kitchen junk drawer?"

"I know I made him clean it out every spring, no matter how much he protested!" Gram smiled at the memory of her husband's stubbornness. "Why do you ask?"

"I found a bunch of boxes full of kitchen drawer junk." Katie chuckled. "I guess he thought he was getting the better of you by just dumping the whole thing into a box every year."

Gram started laughing in earnest now. "Oh, that man," she said. "Never could change his mind about things like that! Well, I suppose he did win that argument in the end, didn't he? Is there anything worth saving in any of the boxes?"

"Not a blessed thing, Gram. I'll be bringing those boxes downstairs in a few minutes. I just needed to cool down a bit. I opened the windows up there, but there's no breeze at all, so it's not helping much."

"Well, if it's too hot, Katie, you could work on the rooms upstairs, instead."

"No, I want to get that attic cleared out, as much as possible, by tonight, before your friend Mr. Branton shows up."

"I'm sure he'll insist that you call him George. He's not a terribly formal person, as I recall." She frowned slightly. "Do you really think you can get that all done by this evening?"

"Yes, I should be able to. As much stuff as there is up there, a lot of it is labeled pretty accurately, and that helps."

"Okay, well, just don't hurt yourself. I'm sure some of those boxes are heavy."

"I'll be fine, Gram." Katie smiled at her grandmother. "I'm a big grown-up woman now, right?" Gram chuckled with her, but there was a hint of sadness around her eyes as she looked at Katie, who was standing up to get back to work.

"Yes, my dear, you are." She sighed quietly and turned back to her crossword puzzle. "Hm... can you think of a seven-letter word for 'dry,' starts with a D?"

Katie thought for a minute, then replied, "Does 'drought' work?"

"It certainly does! Thank you, Katie. I won't hold you any longer."

"No problem, Gram. Let me know if you need any help with dinner, okay?"

"Well, I've got some scallops that I picked up yesterday at the market, so I'll just make my scallops and pasta for you, if that's okay?"

"That sounds wonderful! I can hardly wait." Katie smiled cheerfully. "And with that, I can face the attic again." She put her glass in the sink and headed back upstairs.

After another hour's worth of further effort, she was nearing the halfway point. Among other things, she had found a box of banged-up model trains, which, Katie was certain, had been her father's when he was a boy. Along the eaves, behind the stacks of boxes, she had found a collection of ancient science fair exhibits, some of which still had a collection of ribbons affixed to them.

Katie was beginning to understand a little better why some of this collection was up here. It seemed somehow wrong to just toss her father's boyhood mementoes into a Dumpster, and yet, they had no particular value to anyone else. In the end, she wound up setting a few of the items aside and planned to check with her father the next time they talked to see if he was interested in any of them—which would, she admitted to herself wryly, probably drive her mother up a wall, in her turn.

Finally, she came down to one last crate on the far half of the attic, and she resolved to open the other chest when she returned from carrying this one—full of disco-era vinyl albums—down to the living room. Doubtless, someone would find them irresistible, though she could not imagine why. The music and fashions in her father's teenage years had always baffled her. Hadn't anyone in the 1970s owned a mirror?

Climbing back up the stairs, she felt her excitement building as she pondered what might be in the second trunk. She walked over to it and dropped to one knee to take a closer look at it. Not nearly as interesting as the other one from the outside, it was plain and unadorned, other than the face of a pitted and stout looking lock that she hadn't noticed before, just under the lip of the lid. Hoping for the best, she grasped the lid and pulled, but it did not budge.

Katie sighed and made her way back to the waiting stack of boxes at the center of the attic. She laughed quietly at herself. So much for using *that* for motivation. On the other hand, she knew, she didn't really have time to spend digging through another chest of relics, if she wanted to finish this up today.

By the time Gram called out to Katie that she'd better get washed up for dinner, she was down to perhaps a dozen boxes and crates. She wasn't sure how she was going to get the trunks down the stairs. While there was an old furniture dolly in the garage, she knew that both pieces were too heavy to move without assistance. She sighed as she washed her hands and wiped dust from her face where it had caked in her sweat.

It would be very interesting to see what George made of the contents of the one chest, at least. Realizing how filthy she'd gotten, Katie stuck her tongue out at herself in the mirror and took another dab at her smudged face with the washcloth.

Sitting down at Gram's formal dining table, with the wonderful smell of scallops wafting up from the plate in front of her, Katie was transported to other evenings and other meals here. Grandpa had loved his seafood, and Gram had learned dozens of wonderful recipes to take advantage of their proximity to the ocean.

"Well, Gram, I'm pretty close up there—just another hour or so after dinner, and I should have all but the trunks cleared out."

"That's good, dear. Did you find anything else interesting?"

"No, not really. There was a box of tools that I set in the living room to sell, and I've tossed a couple of boxes of broken electrical appliances. I guess Grandpa planned to fix them up, but most of them probably just weren't worth the effort. Most of the rest of it has been old business records, Dad's old things, and just junk."

"That sounds about right to me, Katy. I never could get Grandpa to toss an old toaster or what have you. He would insist, 'I can just replace this wire, it'll be right as rain again!' and carry it off to the shop. Sometimes, he would come back in hours later with the thing, and it would actually work again." She paused, a gentle smile crinkling the corners of her eyes.

"Of course, as much time as he spent on those things, he could have just bought new ones and still come out ahead."

"Yes, but that wouldn't have been as much fun for him, now would it have been, Gram?"

"No, I suppose not. He always got a charge out of resurrecting a broken thing. He seemed to regard it as a personal victory over disorder, and a blow for frugality." A distant look came over her, and she seemed to shrink down into her chair, as she remembered her lost love.

Katie felt a pang of sympathy for her grandmother. As shocking as it had been to hear the news from her mother when she came home from school that day, as terrible as it had been to see her father's eyes swollen and red before he turned away, she knew that it was nothing in comparison to the loss that Gram still felt.

Gram shook her head, as if clearing her mind, and said, "Would you like some Brussels sprouts, dear? I think that they came out particularly well tonight."

The conversation remained on safer ground as they ate, discussing the logistics of the yard sale and what Katie would work on next, once the attic was emptied.

"I really don't know how I'm going to get those chests out of there, Gram," Katie said. "Also, do you by any chance know where the key to the smaller one might be? I wanted to take a peek in it, too, this afternoon, but it seems to be locked."

"Oh, no, I have no idea where such a thing might be. Perhaps we can ask George when he gets here who he might recommend to help you open it. As far as getting them out of the attic, let's just leave them up there for now and have the movers take them with everything else."

"Oh, of course, Gram. I just got so focused on getting the attic completely cleared out that I forgot about them." Katie laughed at herself. "We should still show them to George, since there are a lot of other things in the large trunk that he might find interesting."

"Certainly, dear. Could you get the cobbler from on top of the stove? It should be cooled down now, and I do believe I'm ready for a bit of dessert."

Katie cleared the dinner dishes and returned with the peach cobbler and plates. "Should I start some coffee to go with it?"

"That would be wonderful, dear. Set out an extra plate and coffee cup for George, too, if you would. He should be along any time now."

Indeed, just as the timer went off for Katie to push the plunger on the French press, he was rapping with the old, black knocker on the door. Gram went to answer it while Katie finished setting out the coffee and cobbler.

She returned to the dining room with George, who was older than Katie had expected, with thin, greying hair and a neatly trimmed beard.

"George, my granddaughter, Katie. Katie, George Branton, who used to work for Grandpa before he returned to the ivy towers." Gram's impish smile was back, and it was clear that this was not the first time she had teased George about his decision to go back into academia.

"Mr. Branton, a pleasure to meet you." Katie extended her hand and was surprised when he bent over it rather than simply shaking it.

"The pleasure is all mine, Miss Harris," he said, his voice deeper than his slender frame would have led her to expect. "Please, though, call me George, all right?"

"Sure thing, George," Katie said, just the tiniest bit flustered. She was not accustomed to having her hand kissed by anyone, least of all a married, older man.

Gram, knowing Katie well enough to catch her brief flush, grinned again and said, "Now, George, you don't need to be all old-fashioned manners; young women these days aren't used to it."

George flashed a smile in return, and the passing awkwardness of the moment evaporated. "Coffee and cobbler, George?" Gram asked.

"You know I would never pass up a chance at your cobbler, Missus Harris, nor would they permit me to retain my tenure if I ever passed up a free cup of coffee."

They sat around the sturdy oaken table and Katie poured the coffee while Gram cut and served the cobbler.

"I am glad to see you so well, Missus Harris. When I heard about Mister Harris, and then your falls, I must admit that I worried over you."

"Well, George, I'm a bit tougher than all that, you know. Still, the reason that Katie came across those papers is that I have finally decided to sell off this old house and take up residence at The Pines, where I can get a little help if I need it."

"Sell the house, Missus Harris? Why, this place has been in the Harris family for as long as anyone around here can remember!" George took a sip of his coffee and lifted his fork, eyeing the cobbler on his plate.

"I know, George, but it can't be helped. Joe's not in any

position to move up here and take it on, and his sister... well, the less said about her, the better. Her new husband would just sell it off to the highest bidder anyway, and probably be gone with the money by sundown. I wish I knew where we went wrong with that girl, but—" She stopped herself. "You probably don't really care about our little family dramas, though."

"I'm just so sorry to hear it, Missus Harris. But I understand that you've got to do what seems best for you, not what other folks want you to do."

"Well, the good news is that cleaning out the attic is what caused Katie to find this stack of papers we wanted you to look over."

"Yes, I can't wait to see those, but I'll want to finish up with the coffee and dessert first."

"Of course, of course." Gram picked up her coffee, sipped it, and nodded approvingly. "Katie, you make an excellent cup of coffee."

"I learned from the best, Gram," Katie smiled back.

George tasted the cobbler, closing his eyes and pausing for a moment to just absorb the flavors. "Missus Harris, for your part, you make an incomparable peach cobbler."

"Thank you, George. Coming from you, that is a high complement. I seem to recall that your wife is a pretty fine cook, herself."

"Indeed she is, Missus Harris. She has been trying to wean me off of my desserts, though, saying that they're bad for my heart or some such nonsense. I get one bad score on my last checkup, and she wants me to give up my chief pleasure at the end of a meal. I ask you, where is the justice in that?"

He smiled appealingly and winked at Gram. "No, in truth, I agree with her, but I do miss a fine peach cobbler such as this one."

"Well, George, we won't wreck your diet by offering you a second serving, then." Gram winked back.

George shifted his attention to Katie. "So, Miss Harris, what can you tell me about where you found these papers?"

Katie hurriedly swallowed the mouthful of cobbler she had been chewing on and replied, "Well, I just opened this large chest in the attic—it's about this wide," she held her hands apart almost at arm's length, "and the lid has a plaque on it, engraved with the name Elizabeth Harris, and 1768. Do you really think that the chest is that old?"

George said, "I'd need to look at the design, but yes, it's possible. A chest like you're describing was not that uncommon at that time, and it certainly would have been passed down from generation to generation. But do go on, please."

"Okay, when I opened it, there were blankets in there, and a box of clothes, and then this satchel, and at least one more like it underneath it—I haven't looked at that one yet."

"Well, so far, nothing that sounds implausible to me, as far as the documents being genuine. Shall we finish up here and have a look at them? Perhaps after that, we can go take a look at the trunk itself, and see what the other satchel has in it?"

Katie nodded, eager to learn more herself. All three tucked into their dessert and finished their coffee without much more conversation, and when their plates were clean, Katie stood and collected them, setting them in the sink.

George asked to use the washroom, so that he could clean

his hands before touching the documents, and emerged wearing surgical gloves.

Gram looked startled. "Gracious, is that really necessary?"

"Missus Harris, I don't want to take any chances. Our hands are naturally covered in all manner of oils, and while we wouldn't notice any damage right now, a researcher a hundred years from now would be cursing our fingerprints if we handled them with our bare hands."

Katie looked concerned and said, "I picked the first two up with my fingertips. I was more worried about breaking the paper, though. I hope I didn't do any harm!"

"Miss Harris, I wouldn't worry too much about it. What's done is done, and I doubt that you could have hurt very much with just a moment's handling. Shall we?"

They all walked into the living room, where the satchel waited on the coffee table. Gram and Katie took their seats on the sofa, and George pulled an armchair over to sit opposite them. Pulling a digital camera out of his pocket, he wordlessly snapped a couple of frames of the satchel as it sat on the table, and then opened the flap to look inside.

His eyes lit up as he pulled the first document from the satchel and started to look it over. "Mmm-hmm, mmm-hmm, very nice, a terrific find, and of some relevance to our earlier discussion, Missus Harris. This is the original deed to a plat of land for a Justin Harris, quite possibly even for this very property. I'll have to study it further, but I think it's possible that this land has been in your family ever since it was first settled. Look, here's a date—March of 1767."

Katie leaned over to see the date that George was pointing

to, and was gratified to see that she'd missed it before because it was written out in Roman numerals—not the sort of thing that would jump out to her untrained eyes.

She closed her eyes for a moment, thinking. "You know, I'm not certain, but I think that Justin Harris might have been Elizabeth Harris's husband. Gram, I'm going to ask Mom to e-mail me that genealogy work she's done."

"That seems like it would be a good idea, dear." Gram pursed her lips as George carefully laid the document on the table and took a series of photos of it, including close-ups of each of the wax seals and the signatures on it. Katie could practically hear Gram thinking that regardless of his intents, he needed to mind his own business on the matter of her plans for the house.

George, now lost in the reverie of a researcher, was oblivious to her reaction, and carefully reached into the satchel for the next document. He examined it for a moment, and then set it down to photograph it, as well. "Just a routine letter to a settler, perhaps this same Justin Harris, from a supplier, confirming an order for dry goods to be delivered on his next trip out to the settlement."

He reached in and withdrew the next document. "Ah. Second page, same letter." He took photographs again, and set it aside.

The fourth page that he withdrew was about the size of half of a sheet of typing paper, and had a wax seal at the bottom with a ribbon embossed into it. George's eyebrows went up as he read it, and he set it on the table with a good deal more reverence than he had the prior documents. Almost to himself, as he started snapping pictures, he muttered, "Military commendation letter, very rare, excellent condition. Signed by Colonel Thompson! Remarkable!"

His hand shook slightly as he moved the document over to the small stack on the table.

The next several documents were more prosaic in nature, and George described each as he looked it over, photographed it, and set it aside.

"Personal correspondence to a relative regarding a property loan."

"Letter from a soldier to his wife."

"Supply requisition, mentions the 'superior tobacco' produced on the Harris plantation."

"Letter instructing a neighbor on what needed to be done to maintain the plantation in the master's absence."

"Hm, now this one's interesting. This is in the same hand, it appears, as that soldier writing to his wife, and this time, he's writing to inform her of casualties in a battle. Maybe during the defense of Charleston? In any case, he writes that he was wounded, but doesn't say how badly."

Katie felt a shudder run down her spine. "This very piece of paper carried the news of death and life-changing injuries back home to wives and mothers... my God, what a thing to have to write!"

George looked at her and nodded. "Not only that, but they had suffered military setbacks that must have looked to those in the field like the end of their struggle. Given that they had been fighting against Crown and country, the only reward that they could look forward to was execution as traitors. To put pen to paper under those circumstances was, itself, an act of bravery and defiance."

Gram leaned forward. "Who is the writer? Is it signed?"

George turned the page over. "Same fellow, this Justin

Harris."

"I knew I married into a good family," Gram smiled at George. "Assuming, of course, that he is actually family."

"It's a pretty good bet, given the surname and the fact that the letter was found in a home that has been in the same family for over two centuries."

Gram nodded. "Shall we see what else is in the satchel?"

"Certainly, Missus Harris. Let me just finish up with this one." George carefully photographed both sides of the letter, and then set it with the other documents.

"Just a few pages left in here." He extracted them and glanced over each. "They look like they're all associated, several pages from a single document."

"More routine stuff, it looks like. This is a plantation ledger... it looks like it dates from the period of the British occupation." He photographed each page and set it aside.

Lifting the satchel upright, he peered inside. "Oh-ho! Now, this is very interesting!" He reached in and extracted three small pieces of paper. "Okay, I am not terribly knowledgeable about this field, but this is currency that was issued by what was called the 'provincial congress'—" He peered at the top slip of paper. "—just a year before the Declaration of Independence."

He arranged the slips of paper on the tabletop and snapped a series of photos. Then he sat up and regarded Gram.

"Missus Harris, I have to tell you, these documents and currency could well have a great deal of value on the collector's market. Again, I don't know specifics, but just what we have here might possibly be worth a substantial sum. You may have options other than selling the property off."

Gram's lips pursed again, and she gave George a short glare this time. "What is it to you, George, whether I sell this place or not?" she demanded.

He met her glare with a steady, earnest gaze. "Missus Harris, I have just seen all too many of these historical old houses go up on the market, only to be purchased by some developer who knocks them down and throws up a row of cheaply built townhouses or some such. I believe strongly that old houses like this are part of what maintains our link to the history of this area. Whenever one of them is destroyed, we lose some portion of our heritage."

He sighed. "I'm really not trying to put myself into your personal affairs—and believe me, I don't like the idea of these wonderful documents winding up on some collector's wall somewhere, or in a vault, locked away from researchers and other people who could use them to construct a clearer picture of the history of this region during the Revolution."

Carefully picking up the stack of documents and the old currency, he slipped the stack back into the satchel. "You have uncovered a really interesting trove of our history, here, and I am thrilled that you asked me to come and take a look at it. Just these pictures"—he tapped his camera—"will be invaluable to my research and that of my students. But I cannot, in good faith, fail to tell you that they represent a financial opportunity that you may not have expected."

Gram relaxed visibly as George spoke. "I understand what you're saying, George, and thank you for your concern. I'm not sure that whatever value these have would be sufficient to let me spend the rest of my days here in my home, but I would appreciate anything that you could find out for me in that regard."

Now it was Gram's turn to sigh. "The problem is that I've already put things in motion. The whole reason that Katie was cleaning out the attic was that I was planning to list the house next week. I've signed papers with the real estate agent, I've made arrangements for the assisted living facility"—Katie grimaced—"and I've dragged Katie up here to help me clear everything out of here so that I can move on."

Katie decided that she needed to speak up now. "Gram, I said I'd come help you, but I've just got to tell you that the idea of you moving out of this place is breaking my heart. You have always been so proud of this house, and how you've kept up the property over the years. I also really hate to see you move into a nurs- I mean, an assisted living situation. Is it possible that you could get by with some kind of in-home assistance? Might the money from these documents be enough to keep you here?"

George held a hand up. "Now, Katie, I don't know exactly what they might be worth on the market. The currency, while somewhat rare, is not unique, though the commendation signed by Thompson may be. Do you know who Thomson was?"

"I think that the name sounds familiar, but I'm not sure," Katie admitted.

"Are you familiar with the story of Carolina Day, June 28th?"

Gram spoke up. "Some battle, during the Revolution, wasn't it?"

"Indeed. Colonel Thompson's forces successfully defended the fort at Sullivan's Island, in the Charleston harbor, from a British naval invasion. It was a pivotal early victory for the American forces, and an amazingly unlikely one, given the situation that they started out in."

George shook his head in reflection. "The battle was marked by a number of amazingly gallant and brave actions, so the fact that your ancestor earned a commendation from him is remarkable enough. Having that commendation in our hands is... well, it's one of the more exciting finds of my academic career."

"So that one might be worth more money, then?" Katie asked.

"All I really know is that I've seen any number of really interesting and unique items like that go into the collector's market, and the prices they've fetched at auction have been well beyond anything that I could afford to put them into my research collection. It is entirely possible that a piece like this—particularly if offered with the context of the rest of the documents—could earn some major attention."

Again, he held up a hand. "But, the truth is, I'm speaking well outside of my area of expertise here. You really want to talk to an auction house, one that specializes in Revolution-period items."

He stood up. "Now, you said that there was another satchel? And other items?"

Katie stood, too. "Yes. They're up in the attic, though."

"Missus Harris, was there anything else I could tell you about the documents we've looked at so far, before I go up to look at the trunk and the rest of the stuff?"

Gram shook her head. "No, I guess I just have to think about some things. If you could give me the name of someone who could help me figure out whether these things are worth what you think they might be, I'd be much obliged."

"Certainly, Missus Harris. I can put you in touch with someone in the morning, all right?"

She nodded. "Go on and see what else there is, then. Mind your head in the attic. Frank was always bashing his skull on the joists up there."

After George and Katie left, Gram quietly reached out and ran her hand over the old leather satchel, thinking.

# Chapter 4

Justin paused as he made his way out to the seedling tobacco field, looking up the ridge at the spring growth on the ash trees. The weather was glorious, truly perfect for a day's hard work, but he still felt an icy clutch of fear in the pit of his stomach.

The latest news from Charles Town had not been encouraging. The hotheaded Patriots had broken into the public magazines in the city, and had seized all of the gunpowder stored there. Justin sympathized with those who wanted to force the Parliament in London to rescind what colonists had taken to calling the "Intolerable Acts."

However, Justin felt that confronting the King's men so aggressively was sure to lead only to greater bloodshed, and would not convince the Parliament of anything. Jeremiah, for his part, was nearly apoplectic at the cheek of the "so-called Patriots," as he referred to them with contempt. His latest letter had been full of invective directed at the faction, particularly in the New England Colonies, that had driven such a wedge between the King and his once-loyal Colonies.

Jeremiah had urged Justin to take note of any of his neighbors whom he suspected of disloyalty to the Crown. "The time for action against these Treasonous Acts is not yet at hand, cousin, but when order is restored to this Colony, we shall want to ensure that justice is served, and the hangman is busy," Jeremiah had written.

Justin, reading the letter, told Elizabeth of Jeremiah's sentiments. "I am not so eager to fill the gallows with men who have been our friends and who have helped us at various times. For that matter, my own heart is far from fully in support of the King's actions and the Parliament's strange amnesia to the fact that the colonists, too, are British subjects."

Elizabeth did not reply, other than to nod thoughtfully.

Justin went on, "The Bostonians cry, 'no taxation without representation,' and that seems to me to have a certain logic. Are not the Colonies entitled to seats in Parliament, instead of having to rely on the good intentions of informal proxies who were obliged first to represent their own subjects in England proper?"

Elizabeth spoke now, saying, "I have heard it said, Justin, that the King is ignoring the great charter under which he rules Britain by denying us our voice in London. I do not know enough of the history of Britain to understand this fully. Is it true that King George must answer to a higher law than his own will?"

"Indeed, Elizabeth, he is bound by the same law that has ruled Britain for hundreds of years. The Magna Carta declares that no British subject should be subject to taxation by the Crown, unless he is represented in Parliament."

"It is very different in France, but then, my family had very good reasons for leaving, too. I will confess that I have not paid very much attention to the governance of the Colonies, other than to be grateful that Britain permitted my people to come here and practice our faith without fear. I worry that the Colonies' confrontation with the King could endanger our position here."

"How so, Elizabeth?"

"Could not the King of France take advantage of our fight with Britain to establish his rule over the British Colonies?"

Justin shook his head, replying with a smile, "King Louis has strived for years to extend his influence over these lands, but it has not availed him at all and has cost him nearly all of his American holdings, as you know."

"Will that not make the new King ever more eager to strike for retribution?"

"Perhaps, but I doubt that France is in any position to effect any such strike, Elizabeth. After all, their treasury has lost the income of all of their fur trade in America, and France is left with only a few scattered islands in the Caribbean, since they had to give the town of New Orleans to the Spanish. Your people need not worry for their safety here, my dear."

He leaned over and kissed her forehead. "In any event, I remain hopeful that King George will see reason and grant us representation in the Parliament. With that, the insurrectionists will no longer have any fuel for their bonfires, and we can all return to being loyal Englishmen."

She embraced him tightly. "I do hope you're right, Justin. It would be a bitter blow to have to flee from yet another French tyrant."

Now, although he still believed that they faced no danger from the French, Justin was not so sure that a permanent rupture with England could be averted. News had just arrived from the Massachusetts Colony of pitched battles, and the British Navy's blockade of Boston was causing the American colonists in that inflamed city ever-greater hardship.

Looking at the young shoots of his new tobacco crop and

breathing in the damp, warm smell of the soil, Justin felt a flash of rage at the stubborn, shortsighted men whose arguments could well make his hard work on the land worthless. If the blockade were extended to Charles Town Harbor, merchants would be unable to bring Carolina tobacco to the snuff makers of London. Then the perishable leaves would have to travel overland to Philadelphia or New York, where they could not command the same prices as London paid.

Justin's gamble of bringing the negro slave to the farm last year to increase his land under cultivation might well backfire, should that happen, and he might even wind up having to give up the farm and return with his young family to rely on the good graces of his Charles Town relations.

His jaw clenched at that thought, but he could think of no good solution to the problem. The land, while fertile and rich, was not suitable to rice or indigo cultivation—the spring on the ridge that fed his creek was reliable, but did not carry that much water. He could try to convert it to food production, or perhaps even raising mutton, but he doubted that he could keep cattle.

He turned on his heel and returned to the house. "Elizabeth, I think that we should consider asking Leonard Gauthier up the road if we could purchase some of his lambs, after all. We have enough pasture, I think, to support perhaps a dozen ewes, and it would provide us with another potential source of income, in case the tobacco market should encounter... difficulties."

Elizabeth paused in her sewing and looked thoughtfully into the distance for a moment. "Do you think that Gauthier would part with them in exchange for some turkeys or perhaps pasturage for some of his flock? Since the new paper currency's been issued, I've been trying to avoid taking money, so we haven't very much of it."

"I can ask him. He might even want some tobacco for his pipe, you know."

"That's a good thought, vile as that thing is. I am glad, even though we raise the plant, that you don't use it. I simply cannot abide its smoke."

Justin chuckled. "I know, dear. I like the smell of the leaves as they cure, but I also prefer snuff over a pipe."

Elizabeth smiled at her husband. "And I am glad for that, too, my dear. Yes, do speak with Gauthier, and see what he would take in trade. I agree that it is probably wise for us to have something to fall back on, given the events last month in Massachusetts."

"Very well, I'll go visit him this afternoon, after Terrance and I have the upper field planted." Justin kissed his wife again and started for the door.

"Papa?" Timothy stood up from where he'd been playing in front of the fireplace. "If you get lambs, can I name them?"

Justin laughed, "Perhaps, if you name them 'Stew,' and 'Chops' and 'Fillet.'"

"We're going to eat them, Papa?" Timothy's eyes widened in horror and began to fill with tears. "I want to play with them, Papa, forever and ever! I don't want to eat the lambs!"

"Oh, come here, child," said Elizabeth, gathering the boy into her arms. "Sweetheart, sheep were put on the earth to serve people, first through their wool, which we spin into yarn and make into warm things to wear, and then through their meat, which keeps us strong and healthy so that we may serve the Lord. You like mutton, don't you?"

Timothy stopped sniffling as he considered the question. Slowly, he said, "Yes, Mama, I like meat. But can't we just ask the sheep to give us some meat, without having to slaughter them?"

Justin, trying to avoid upsetting his son even more, stifled his laugh and said, "Timothy, I suppose we can try that. But sheep aren't very smart, and I don't think that they would understand us. Not only that, but your Mama is right—sheep know their place in the world, and the Lord's purpose for them is not merely to serve as our playthings, any more than He put turkeys here just for you to chase through the fields."

Timothy froze, and then started crying anew. "You eat the *turkeys*, too?" he wailed into his Mama's shoulder. Justin bowed his head and closed his eyes for a moment. "Elizabeth, I think I'm going to just go, before I make things any worse..."

Elizabeth, holding Timothy tight and comforting him, smiled and shook her head ruefully at Justin. "Yes, I think that may be for the best."

As Justin left, he could hear Timothy sobbing, "Is that what happened to Wobble-Chin? Did we *eat* him? Did you make *me* eat him?" Justin was glad to escape the house and leave the boy in the care of somebody competent to explain the facts of life to him, hopefully without upsetting him even more.

When he reached the tobacco patch, Justin noted with satisfaction that the negro slave Terrance, whom Jeremiah had loaned him, had already moved almost half of the young tobacco plants to their hillocks in the field that stretched uphill from the house towards the ridge. Despite Jeremiah's disdain for the negro, Justin had found him to be a quick study of the methods and processes on the upland farm.

For his part, Terrance seemed to be happy with his temporary new master. Justin, despite Jeremiah's admonition to "be free with the whip to ensure that that negro doesn't get soft up there on your farm," did not feel that harsh measures were the best means to get the most work out of a slave. Rather, he took the approach of working hard to inspire Terrance to follow his own good example in the fields.

Respect, not fear, was necessary on a farm where there was no overseer, where a fearful slave might decide that his lot could be improved by making a break for freedom, and might even be further improved by leaving none behind to pursue him. Justin was aware that his pale skin did not make him safe from the potential of harm, and so his own minor level of fear guided his actions in disagreeing with Terrance's owner.

"Ho there, Terrance," Justin greeted the black-skinned man, as Terrance made his way back up from the field. "Good work already this morning. We should be done with this field by mid-day!"

Terrance smiled quickly and bent to lift another tobacco plant from the soil, choosing a healthy, robust stem over its smaller or damaged neighbors. His nimble fingers gently separated the root ball from the loose soil in which it had germinated and spent the past couple of months. He carried it to the next mound in a row of hillocks, and carefully set it into the top of the mound, pressing the soil down around the roots.

He splashed a bit of water from the bucket next to the hillock onto the transplanted seedling, and moved up the row, stooping to pick up the heavy hoe he would use to raise the next mound. Justin easily fell into the same routine on the next row, and the two men worked side-by-side for hours, barely exchanging more than a few words the entire time.

Justin knew that Jeremiah would have a sharp tongue if he saw his cousin working alongside the negro slave under the springtime sun, but he had considered the matter when Terrance had first arrived at the farm. While it might appeal to a man of Jeremiah's nature to take his leisure while he watched others labor in his fields, Justin was more pragmatic about the contributions that another set of hands could make.

Since his motivation for accepting the loan of the slave was to increase his farm's income for what they could not raise themselves, it would have been folly for Justin to simply substitute the slave's labor for his own. Furthermore, by working with the black man, rather than over him, Justin was able to easily accomplish things that he would have had to ask his neighbors for assistance with previously.

Near the main house, a new tobacco house stood, ready to accommodate the larger harvest from the additional fields. With Terrance's help, Justin had been able to fell the trees, clearing the new fields in the process, cut the logs into rough planks and posts, and erect the rude—but sturdy—structure in just a matter of weeks, and even had it ready in time for last fall's harvest.

As he had grown to know Terrance better, too, he had come to appreciate the other man's intelligence. Terrance had looked at the wooded slope that Justin had initially planned to clear, and had pointed out that the spring above it was surpassed in volume by one just a little further down the ridge from the house. Once the trees were reduced to stumps, and the brush cleared away, Justin was glad that the other man had spoken up. Though it had meant a bit more work initially, irrigation would be far easier, and the tobacco healthier, in this location.

Terrance's experience working on a larger plantation had been invaluable in the construction of the tobacco house, too. Justin had only to explain what size of covered area he wanted, and Terrance had set to work, digging post holes for the foundation, and selecting and laying out the trunks that they would split for the timbers the structure would need.

As Justin had predicted, they were nearly finished with the field when Elizabeth emerged from the house to call them in for dinner. The two men walked back together and crouched by the stream side by side as they rinsed the soil from their hands and from under their fingernails.

"We did good work today, boss," said Terrance in his gravelly voice. "I didn't think we'd get it all done by now, but you were right."

"I've been doing this for a long time, Terrance," Justin replied. "I know how long that field would have taken me, so I just figured how long it would have taken three of me to get it done." He smiled at the other man. "You are a good worker, and I'm glad that you were able to come and help us."

Terrance smiled, this time more broadly, and rose, wiping his hands on the relatively cleaner flanks of his rough pants. "Thank you kindly for saying so, boss. This work is a whole lot more pleasant than wading through the indigo fields or the rice swamps. I'm glad to be here."

Justin joined him and the two men walked down to the house together, where Elizabeth waited with the children to start their midday meal.

# Chapter 5

As they climbed the stairs back into the close and musty air of the attic, Katie was aware that she could not seem to stop herself from chattering at George.

"I had no idea, when I was a kid running around up here, that I was so close to so much history," she bubbled. "I mean, I knew that the city had been around for hundreds of years, but I'd never really thought about how old the house was. Can you tell, looking at it, when it was built?"

George found the young woman's excitement infectious. "That's pretty well outside my area of expertise, but I'm sure that we can find out how old the house is pretty easily from the tax records."

As they came to the top of the stairs, he continued, "It's always been amazing to me what comes out of some folks' attics. Of course, I don't often get the opportunity to go up into them personally, so this is exciting for me."

"There's the trunk," Katie said, pointing. She led the way and they walked, stooped over, in single file through the peak of the room to where it awaited.

She knelt in front of the heavy old hasp and waited while George dropped to one knee beside her, and took out the camera again. He snapped a photo of the entire trunk, and a close-up shot of the plaque, before she opened the heavy lid. George spent a minute shifting this way and that, taking more pictures and trying to get a clear look at the contents, despite the harsh shadows cast by the single naked bulb behind them.

Finally, he reached in and started examining the contents. He glanced at the blankets and shrugged to Katie. "I really don't know anything about quilts, but we should probably take these downstairs so that I can get some pictures and send them to a lady I know who is very well-regarded in that field. These could be from the same period as the letters, or they could be from the 1970s. She'll know right away."

"Okay," Katie said and took the pile from him as he lifted it out. She stood and started for the stairs. "I'll just bring these down to the guest room, and be right back."

"Sounds good." George turned his attention back to the trunk itself, snapping pictures of the hardware on it, until Katie reappeared at the stairway.

"The rest of the trunk does seem to be consistent with the plate on the top. It's a pretty remarkable piece, though, again, it's outside of my direct field of knowledge."

"Then let's take a look at the part that you do know about, shall we?" Katie reached in for the satchel that lay beneath the one they'd already looked through. This one seemed to be constructed of a dense canvas and had a stout buckle on it, holding it shut. Wordlessly, she handed it over to George, who sat back on his heels and cradled it in his lap for a moment.

He took a deep breath, blew it out, and said, "Well, here goes. No, wait a sec." He grabbed his camera again, and took a series of photos of the satchel. That done, he set it upright on his knees and started to undo the buckle. It resisted, corrosion holding the clasp to the grommet on the strap.

George grunted as the strap came free, then proceeded more gently, sliding the buckle apart and opening the top flap. Katie could see a jumble of envelopes within, and her heart leapt in her chest as George extracted the stack.

"At a glance, I am pretty sure that these are a good deal later than the other satchel's contents." He quickly leafed through the top of the stack.

"They look like 20th century letters, mainly. Some World War I dates, some from the Depression era, and the bulk of them seem to be from the '40s and '50s."

Katie sighed with disappointment.

George smiled at her. "Trust me, this stuff can be even more interesting than the Revolutionary-era documents, since you'll know some of the people who wrote and received these. They're just not as likely to have great historical value."

"Yeah, I just got all excited by that first bunch of documents. Is there anything else in here?" She leaned over and peered into the chest.

"George?" She couldn't see clearly, but there was a stack of loose papers, and they were similar in appearance to the documents that had come out of the first satchel.

George reached past her with his gloved hand, and pulled the papers out. On top was a sheet of thin, deeply yellowed paper, covered with closely spaced printing in two neat columns. Katie could make out an ornate seal at the top, and the words "CAPE-FEAR MERCURY" surrounding it.

As George's eyes fell upon the page, Katie saw them widen

suddenly, followed by all of the color draining from his face. His jaw dropped as he continued reading. Then he looked up at her. His mouth worked, but no sound came out.

Eventually, George quit gasping like a beached fish and took a deep breath. His color improved a bit, and he set the papers down on the corner of the chest with a visibly shaky hand before he spoke. "This... document. It's something that historians of the Carolinas have dreamed of having for... well, centuries. Have you heard of the Mecklenburg Declaration?"

"I can't say that I have, no."

George shifted into the tone of a practiced lecturer. "Okay, well, it happened just after the battles of Lexington and Concord, which took place in Massachusetts, of course, April of 1775, and really marked the beginning of open hostilities between the British soldiers and the colonials. News of these battles reached Charlotte in May, just as a group calling itself the 'Committee of Safety' was meeting, planning to draw up instructions for the North Carolina delegation to the Continental Congress."

Again, he had to draw a deep breath and pause for a moment. "Now, what I have been taught, and have taught in turn, was that those instructions were relatively radical, and that they were much later—forty years later—misremembered as having included an actual declaration of independence from Britain, more than a year before Jefferson's Declaration. The original records were lost in a fire around 1800, which made corroborating this claim impossible."

He nodded meaningfully toward the papers resting on the corner of the chest, and Katie could hear a quaver in his voice as he said, "If I can substantiate the circumstances under which these papers came to be in this trunk and prove their authenticity, though, we will have the proof of that declaration, including its original text."

He stood and picked up his camera again. "This is a find of extraordinary importance, and so I need to document everything about its environment very carefully, all right?"

Katie nodded, and he began snapping a seemingly endless series of pictures of the attic, the chest and the papers themselves, chattering away as he did so. "There's already been one hoax—involving, ironically, this same broadsheet. But I have a strong feeling that this is no hoax. Unless you're a mastermind of Revolution-era forgeries?" He looked at Katie with a playful twinkle in his eye.

She laughed, "No, not at all! I'm in pre-med over at Emory. What I know about Revolutionary history would make for a short essay, and not even an A-grade one."

He smiled back at her and continued, "These papers will help our understanding of how the idea of independence from Britain grew from just a few hotheads griping about esoteric tax theory and Scottish philosophy into a movement that swept the Colonies into a war with the greatest military force on the planet at the time."

He smiled wryly at Katie. "When you think about it, they were nuts to do it. We can talk about long, thin supply lines, geopolitical circumstances, even climate variations, all of which aided the cause of independence to one extent or another, but the objective truth of the matter is that in the early 1770s, nobody would have given you odds of the Colonies being able to wage a successful war of secession from Mother Britain. Everything appeared to be stacked against them, yet they prevailed."

Returning to the papers, he started taking careful pictures

of both sides of each sheet, even when they appeared to be blank. "These documents could be instrumental in helping us to understand how this came about. I'm not exaggerating when I say that this is the sort of find that every historian dreams of coming across at some point in his or her career."

He shook his head slowly, wonderingly. "And here it is, in the attic of an old house where my former boss grew up and lived his life. Practically under my nose all these years. Unbelievable."

# Chapter 6

J ustin sat next to his cousin Jeremiah on the broad verandah of his plantation home, a generous supper filling his belly, a glass of sack in his hand, and a blue haze of smoke from Jeremiah's fashionable "seegar" thick in the air around the two men. Jeremiah was expounding upon his favorite subject these days, the foolishness of the "so-called *Patriots* of these Colonies."

"They could have prosperity and peace, and sleep soundly at night, secure in the knowledge that they were faithfully serving their sovereign. Instead, they choose to pick apart some two-farthing bit of legal philosophy and blow it up into a matter that good men are dying over today!"

Jeremiah's fierce eyes and reddened face left no doubt as to on which side the good men he lamented had fallen. "In the scheme of all things, what are a few pennies of tax, and how can any reasonable man declaim our responsibility to pay our share toward the defense that the King has put up on our—*our!*—behalf here in these Colonies? Why, without the Royal Navy, I don't doubt that the New England colonists should all be learning to speak French even now."

Rising into a full fury now, Jeremiah shouted, loudly enough that the hands in the field looked up for a moment to see whether they were the target of his rage. "And how would they like that, with their Scottish 'Enlightenment' philosophies and their fancies of an independent destiny?" He spat with impressive force and vehemence over the rail of the porch. Justin sat silently, looking into his glass of wine and waiting for the older man's bluster to run out.

"And have you heard of what those fools up in North-Carolina have done?" Jeremiah shouted, veins starting to stand out on his forehead. "Just a moment, I'll show you." He rose ponderously from his chair, and walked briskly inside, returning in a moment with a broadside, which he waved viciously in the air.

"Look at this outrage! It's bad enough that the fools in Boston City have provoked His Majesty's troops into firing upon traitors, but now those in Mecklenburg County up in North-Carolina Colony want to visit the Crown's righteous wrath upon the citizens of that place, as well. Read this for yourself." He shoved the newspaper in Justin's direction, and the younger man gingerly took it.

As Justin read, his heart began to hammer in his chest. Independency from Britain! Styling themselves masters of a separate and equal nation before God! No wonder Jeremiah was so exercised.

"I've done my part for the King, though," said Jeremiah, looking satisfied with himself. "I dispatched a man to buy up every copy of that filth from Charlotte Town and dispose of it, lest it infect other localities with the same insanity." Justin started to hand the offending paper back to his cousin, but Jeremiah waved the broadside away.

"No, keep it, if you like. There is other news in there, as well, and I know how rarely you get any sense of life in the civilized world out on your farm. I trust that you will not fall prey to the nonsense chronicled there, and you may well benefit from seeing what fools some of our countrymen have become."

"Thank you kindly, cousin," said Justin, tucking the newspaper into the traveling bag by his feet. "I shall ensure that it is kept out of the sight of more impressionable men in my district."

"Very good. I knew you had a good head on your shoulders. Not like these blockheads who are agitating the Colonies into open rebellion against our King. I never thought I'd see the day when my indigo would be unwelcome at the docks of London, and our own ships suffer under threat of blockade."

*Now we get to the crux of the matter*, thought Justin, but he wisely kept his thoughts to himself. Jeremiah, apparently tired of fulminating against the insurrectionists, changed the subject abruptly. "I am glad to read by your last letter that the negro slave I have loaned you has helped you with your production on the farm."

"He is a wondrous good worker, Jeremiah, and I am much in your debt for the kind assistance you have shown me through his labor."

Jeremiah harrumphed and said, "He was never all that industrious in the indigo or rice fields. Perhaps he just needed the closer supervision that you can give him. I trust that you have a neighbor keeping close watch over him in your absence?"

"Indeed I do," Justin replied. Though he did not actually feel that the negro's disposition warranted such distrust, he knew that Jeremiah would worry overly if he were not assured of the safety of the family on the farm. "Additionally, Elizabeth is, of course, fully comfortable in the use of a firearm to defend herself, should the need ever arise, and we make the negro sleep out in the tobacco house when I am absent from the farm."

"Very good, very prudent," said Jeremiah. "If your tobacco crop is of large enough quantity this year, perhaps you could consign to me four hogsheads and take title to the negro as your own?" He drew on his seegar, the tip lighting his face in the deepening shadows of the evening.

Justin was taken aback for a moment, considering the generosity of the offer. A prime negro was easily worth half again what Jeremiah was proposing, and Justin had found Terrance to be worth well more than might be expected of even a top-quality buck slave.

Four hogsheads could easily represent the entire production of the farm this year, but given the uncertainty of the market in the face of a potential expansion of the British blockade to include the ports of the Southern Colonies, Justin came to the snap decision that it was worth the risk.

He put out his hand to his cousin. "'Tis a bargain," he said, enthusiastically.

"It is no loss to me, cousin," Jeremiah replied. "My negroes have increased faster than they have fallen, and I cannot easily find any more land to employ them on." He sighed dramatically. "Unlike you folk in the open countryside, there is no untamed wild here to claim, and we are left to purchase from one another when we desire to improve our holdings."

He drew on his seegar again. "In any event, given that my overseer informs me that that particular negro was less productive than many for me, I am glad enough to be rid of him, particularly as you have found him to be well suited to your needs. I shall draw up the bill of sale for you, as well as a detailing of our agreement."

"Is that necessary, cousin? I know that such documents come dear in these days," Justin protested.

"I have found, through long and bitter experience, that it is more important in dealing with family than even with strangers, to have the clarity of a written agreement, for the protection and security of all parties involved."

His eyes twinkled as a mercenary grin appeared on his face. "As to the cost, I expect to be able to sell the tobacco up North, should trade with the mother country be interrupted by the intransigence of our 'Patriot' friends. A new factory has lately been established in Philadelphia City, and if they should cost me the trade, why should they not bear the responsibility for replacing it?"

Justin nodded and smiled in return. "Why not, indeed, cousin?"

Jeremiah, tossing back the remainder of his wine, said, "So, are you still determined to leave tomorrow, then, Justin?"

"Yes, I want to get back home and see to the farm. This may be the season when the sun and the rain do the majority of the work, but a farmer's tasks are never ending, even so."

"True enough," Jeremiah grimaced. "Wait until your plantation has grown to the size of mine, and you'll find that no season offers a respite from the work. Of course," Jeremiah chuckled, "by then, you'll have such a stable of negroes that you'll be like me, and most of your difficulties will be in simply making sure that everyone is doing what you've asked them to do."

Jeremiah sighed, took a last draw on the seegar and tossed it to the ground, where a thin line of smoke drifted aromatically up from it until the coal winked out. "Well, cousin, I believe I will retire now. We'll breakfast together, and I'll get those papers drawn up so that we may sign them before you leave."

Justin nodded, "That sounds good." He shook the older man's hand. "Thanks again for your hospitality, and for your generosity. I only hope that someday I can match both."

Jeremiah waved dismissively. "It's nothing, really." He stood, and inclined his head at Justin. "I have a feeling that you will surpass my hospitality and my generosity both, in time. You are a fine young man, and I make a special point of helping such as yourself get their start."

He turned to go inside. "Sleep soundly, cousin. I shall see you when we breakfast in the morning."

Justin sat out in the deepening twilight for a while longer. A negro house slave brought out a lantern and returned inside without saying a word. Pondering on the future and his cousin's words, Justin hoped that events would permit him the success that Jeremiah had achieved.

Finally, he stood and snuffed the lantern as he went inside, himself.

Breakfast the next morning was an uncharacteristically raucous time. Jeremiah's wife and children joined them in the kitchen for the morning meal.

Justin was completely unable to keep all of their names straight, but he was pretty sure there were six of them in total, ranging from the solemn Jane, who was nearing the bloom of her womanly youth, to the rambunctious twins Ezra and Ephraim— "Ez and Eph," Jeremiah called them—who were probably the same age as Justin's Timothy.

Jeremiah's wife, Anna, was a surprisingly energetic woman, who ruled over her children with the assistance of a young Irish servant—"her indenture cost us near half what a negro would have cost to buy outright, but at least she speaks English, after a fashion," Jeremiah muttered to Justin.

Justin enjoyed visiting with the children, though they did make him miss his own three more than ever. Once the meal was over, Jeremiah and Justin signed the contract for Terrance's sale, and Justin was free to set off on the familiar journey home. Though he knew that it would leave the farm short on cash for the next year or so, Justin was confident that his investment would prove worthwhile.

# Chapter 7

George carried the precious newspaper downstairs before him, balanced on the flats of his palms. When they reached the living room, he set them down on the coffee table.

"Missus Harris, I believe that this represents a discovery of monumental importance for our understanding of the Revolutionary era here in the Carolinas. In a nutshell, this is proof of an event whose veracity has been debated by historians from Thomas Jefferson to the present day. Perhaps you learned about the Mecklenberg Declaration of Independence?"

"Why yes, I do seem to recall one of my history teachers in high school making a fuss about it in the spring one year. Some folks in North Carolina who weren't waiting for the New England lawyer types to get around to break away from Britain, and did it themselves well before the official Declaration?"

"That's the one, Missus Harris... and this provides conclusive evidence of that earlier Declaration. If I can authenticate it, we will also finally have the text of that resolution, as it was passed, rather than as it was recalled later."

"How would such a thing have come to rest in my house, George?"

"That I cannot answer yet, but it will be a crucial question as we work on proving that this is actually the newspaper that contemporary accounts claimed had printed the Declaration and its story. For now, though, my top priority needs to be the preservation of this document. I need to get some materials from my car, and I'll be right back.

George returned in a few moments with a stack of special folders—"acid-free, specially treated for storing historical documents," he explained, and carefully slid each page of the broadside into a separate folder. Once the document was securely stored, he seemed to start breathing somewhat normally again.

"I would like to make a quick telephone call, if I might," he said, reaching into his pocket and pulling out his cell phone. Gram nodded and motioned her approval, and he dialed quickly.

"Kevin, hi, sorry for calling this late, but I know you're going to want to hear this," he said into the phone. "I'm at the house of an old friend of mine, and we were going through some documents that she had found here. You're not going to believe what I'm looking at."

He flipped open the folder containing the front page of the newspaper, and read off, "The *Cape-Fear Mercury*, Wednesday, June 7, 1775." Continuing to the headline, he read, "A Resolution Adopted in Charlotte Town on May 20th, Declaring Mecklenberg County to be Free and Independent from the Nation of Britain."

There was silence for a moment, and then Katie could hear the excited tones of George's colleague as he first whooped into the phone, causing George to hold the instrument away from his ear with a pained expression, and then started asking questions a mile a minute.

George tried to keep up, "Yes, I found it in a trunk, under some contemporaneous documents and some later ones," then,

"It's it pretty good shape—some browning and edge damage, but the bulk of it is pretty good." He paused and listened for a moment. "All four pages were present, yes.... Yes, that will help with the authentication, too."

He smiled at Gram and Katie and held up his hand, nodding into the telephone. "Okay, Kevin, yes, I'll bring it in tonight. Okay... all right, I'll see you there. Okay, bye." He snapped the phone shut and replaced it in his pocket. "As I thought, my colleague wants to see this right away. Missus Harris, is it all right with you if I bring this to the University for the time being? I assure you that we will take good care of it for you."

"Certainly, George—this is why I called you in the first place. It sounds like you need to go right now, which is fine, yes, take it with you, please. Call us in the morning and let us know if you learn anything new about it, okay?"

"Most certainly Missus Harris." He stood and gathered the folders, carefully setting them into the box they had come in.

"Thank you so very, very much for this, Missus Harris. I can't tell you what it means to me that you asked me to come and take a look at these. Even if it had all turned out to be just common stuff, I really appreciate the chance to see you again and to have a look at what you have here."

"It's no great thing, George. Frank always did speak highly of you, and I'm just happy that you found something interesting." George nodded gratefully and turned to Katie.

"Katie, it has been a pleasure meeting you, never mind what we found upstairs. I will have to come back, of course—there's still that other trunk up there—but I will probably be a few days working on this. I'll keep you both updated."

"Thank you, George. I'm excited to hear more details about all of this. Let me give you my e-mail address, too, okay?" They exchanged information, and then George turned to leave.

"Thanks again, ladies. I'll call in the morning!"

After the door closed behind him, Katie sat down opposite Gram and blew her breath out gustily. "Wow, I thought we had some kind of interesting stuff up there, but nothing like this!"

Gram chuckled. "Just goes to show that sometimes the packrats get it right."

"No kidding," Katie replied, laughing. "My gosh, I think I might have trouble ever throwing away a newspaper or a letter again!"

"Now, Katie," her grandmother admonished, her eyes crinkled with laughter, "Don't forget about all of the *other* boxes you had to drag down from there to get at those few pages!"

"True, Gram, good point. Still... it makes me wonder what we toss on a routine basis that might turn out later to be the crucial missing data point for some historian."

Later, as she lay in the same room she had spent summers in as a teenager, looking at the shadows cast by a streetlight around the edges of the blind on the window, Katie thought again about the letters she had held in her hands that morning.

Although she understood the historical importance of the newspaper and appreciated why it excited George so much, somehow the pages that had known the pen of her own ancestors made her feel more connected with her past. The thought that their hands had held those pages, that a wife had wept over the news they contained, that a new venture had begun, perhaps on the very same land she had roamed as a child, recorded on those pages, moved her deeply.

When she finally did get to sleep, she dreamed of the men and women who had lived through those days, and what had carried them through the darkness of war and the confusion of change.

# Chapter 8

Justin rode the last few miles to home feeling uncharacteristically at ease. He knew he had taken a gamble, but he couldn't help but feel certain that he'd done the right thing for everyone involved. Sometimes, he knew, boldness was required in order to achieve greatness.

As he came over the rise to his farm, he instantly felt that something was amiss. He spurred his tired mare into a full gallop and leaped out of the saddle as soon as she stopped in front of the house. As he entered, and his eyes adjusted to the relative darkness inside, he realized what had alerted him—no fire burned in the grate.

However, he was relieved to see Elizabeth and the children seated at the table. His wife, looking wan and red-eyed, sat holding Katherine in her arms. The toddler was bundled up and sucking her thumb, her solemn dark eyes sunken in her face. The baby lay in his cradle, his legs waving cheerfully in the air, in counterpoint to the somber look on Timothy's face.

"Whatever has happened here?" Justin exclaimed, his voice breaking as he crossed the room to embrace his wife and daughter.

Elizabeth drew a long shuddering breath and answered, "There was a s-s-snake, Justin. She was playing by the creek and didn't see it, and it— it— it bit her." She began to weep now, leaning into Justin's arms and taking comfort in his presence.

Timothy spoke up now. "Terrance, he got to her first, Papa. He knew just what to do. He killed the snake with a stick, then he brought her up to the house and cleaned all of the poison out of her foot with his mouth. He did it so fast we didn't even know what was the matter until he was asking us for cloth to bandage where he had to cut her. "

Justin looked, wonderingly, at Elizabeth, who nodded confirmation of the boy's story, while continuing to sob and rock Katherine.

"May I see?" Justin gently unbundled his daughter's legs, finding the expertly-tied bandage on her chubby left leg. Her foot was badly swollen, but he noted with relief that the swelling did not seem to extend beyond where the bandage was wrapped tightly around her calf.

Bending to kiss his daughter's forehead, he asked, "Where is Terrance now?"

Timothy answered, "He's out tending the tobacco, Papa. He said that there wasn't anything more he could do for Katherine, and that the work still needed doing."

Justin shook his head slowly in wonder. There was no doubt in his heart at all now that he had done the right thing in Charles Town.

"I'm going to go and speak to him now, Timothy. Can you see to laying a fire in the hearth, so that we can get something cooking?"

"Yes, Papa. I'm sorry that—"

"No, you did fine, Timothy. Mama and the babies needed you in here with them, but now that I'm home, it's all going to be all right." Justin stood and took a deep breath. "Everyone did just fine, and I'm proud of all of you."

He walked out to the lower field, where Terrance was stooped, picking the lower leaves off of the tobacco plants to ensure that only the topmost leaves would take up sustenance from the soil and that they would grow large and strong in the sun.

"Terrance," Justin called across the field. Terrance stood and waited, a neutral expression on his face. Justin strode up to him.

"Terrance, I— I wanted to thank you. You saved my little girl, and I—" His eyes welled up with unshed tears, and he reached out, placing his hand on the other man's shoulder. Then, to his surprise, he found himself pulling the negro into a tight embrace.

Terrance stood stiffly for a moment, shocked, and then brought his hand up to pat Justin's back softly. "You're welcome, Mister Harris," he said, his deep voice grave. "I only did what needed to be done."

Justin released him, feeling the first hints of a deep disquiet at the fact that this negro—this *man*—who had done his family such an extraordinary service was subject to an agreement to become his... property, like a prized bull, or a fine dog.

Terrance continued, "I saw a little boy get bit like that back at your cousin's plantation, and my father, he did the same as what I did for little Katherine. Is she still doing all right?"

"You did just perfectly, Terrance. Thank you. I... I don't know what to say."

"I reckon you've said what needed saying, Mister Harris. And you're welcome." Terrance turned and went back to his work, the sun shining back at Justin from the fine sheen of sweat on the negro's back.

Justin, unsure of what else he could add, slowly turned and walked back toward the house. He went through the motions of taking the tack off of the mare and rubbing her down from her long day's journey, and then went back inside.

There, he started the fire that Timothy had laid, and then took Katherine from Elizabeth so she could get a meal started. He cradled his daughter, and she stirred uncomfortably a few times in his arms, but, aside from an occasional sniffle, she seemed to be all right.

Justin watched as Elizabeth moved about the cooking area quietly, her eyes still red and bright but her motions efficient and practiced. "That negro is a fine man," Justin finally said.

Elizabeth turned to him. "He saved my little girl, Justin. How can we ever repay that? Your cousin doesn't know what an asset he has in Terrance, but I surely hope that you can prevail upon Jeremiah to reward him somehow."

"Well," said Justin, "about that. Jeremiah made me a very kind offer while I was there, and I accepted it. Terrance will be ours after the harvest. My cousin wanted four hogsheads of tobacco for him, which is likely to be nearly all we produce this year, even with the new fields, but that's a better price than he could have gotten for the negro on the block, far better."

Elizabeth absorbed this information for a moment, and then replied, "I think you made a good decision, Justin. We have a little money still left from last harvest, and the sheep should show a small profit, as well, this year, if their wool is as good quality as Gauthier claimed it would be."

She turned back to the skillet in which she was frying up some pork. "You're doing a good thing, too, taking Terrance off of Jeremiah's plantation. I do believe that he likes the work here better, and I am certain that we treat him better than he got back in Charles Town. Have you told him yet?"

"No, I— I thought I should tell you, first," Justin said. In truth, he hadn't wanted to speak to the negro about a change in his ownership in the same breath as thanking him for what he'd done. Justin was starting to wonder, too, whether the broadsides that had made their way to the village from Quakers in the northern Colonies might have some truth to them.

Saying that negroes were human beings, not some lesser beast, Justin could agree with readily enough. The call for universal freedom for all slaves, though, he could not see how that could work. His little farm would never grow without the benefit of slave labor, and a plantation like Jeremiah's would collapse utterly without the negroes.

No, the Quakers, like so many who lived their lives in philosophy and reflection, and never stirred out into the real world to see how things operated, did not understand the necessity of slavery to the success of the southern Colonies. While the theory had a certain attraction, Justin knew the actuality of abolishing slavery would mean ruin for this society.

Katherine stirred again in his arms and pulled her thumb out of her mouth. "My ouchie hurts, Papa. That 'nake bited me, and it hurt. Terrance hit the bad 'nake and carried me back here." She thought for a long moment, her eyes solemn, and added, "Papa, I never saw Terrance cry before. Did the 'nake hurt him, too?"

Justin took a moment to recover his composure after this revelation, and after a moment, he replied, "No, sweetie, the snake didn't bite Terrance, but he was scared for you, just like Mama and

Papa. But he took good care of you, and we're going to, also." He kissed her forehead again, and held her close to him, swaying to comfort her.

That night, as he settled down to sleep, Justin listened to the slow, steady snores coming from Terrance's pallet on the other side of the room and dropped off to sleep thinking about the events of the day and what they might portend.

# Chapter 9

Gram's homemade biscuits and gravy were just as good as Katie remembered, and with that substantial breakfast to sustain her, she returned to the attic to finish clearing out the remainder of the boxes. She happened to be passing through the kitchen when the phone rang. George had an initial report on the broadsides he'd taken to the university the night before.

Katie leaned her head close to Gram's as the older woman held the phone so they could both hear what George said.

"So far, Missus Harris, the newspaper seems to check out in every way that we've looked at. I've found a fellow up in Charlotte who has examined most every copy of the *Mercury* known to have survived, and he's flying down this afternoon to have a look at this one. From what he was able to tell me to look for over the phone, he's pretty convinced that this is the real thing."

"That's wonderful, George," Gram said. "After he looks at it, what will you do next, assuming that he agrees that it's real?"

"Well, once it's authenticated, we'll have to prepare a statement for the press. Missus Harris, if you want, I can try to keep your name out of it, but I can't guarantee that they won't find out at some point. I'll warn you, though... it's going to be a circus. I wouldn't be at all surprised if this were on the national news tomorrow."

"Goodness," said Gram, bringing her hand up to her mouth.

Katie's eyes were wide, too, and she couldn't help but give Gram an excited little grin.

"George, I think we can handle the attention, if it comes to that," Gram finally said. "You know that Frank wouldn't have wanted me to hide away if something as exciting as this had happened while he was still with us."

"Missus Harris, I do believe that you're right about that. I'll try to make sure we have someone from the university's PR office available to you, so if things get too wild, we can help you out. Uh, you might want to take your phone off the hook, though, at least when you want to sleep." He gave a nervous little laugh, and Gram smiled.

"Don't you worry about me, George. I suspect that even a reporter from a big, fancy national television show will think twice about tangling with me, if I give him what-for."

"Right you are, Missus Harris. Frank would come into the shop some days saying that he should have just spent the night under his desk, you had dressed him down so thoroughly for one thing or another. And you *liked* him... some of those reporters, I doubt even their own mothers like 'em." George laughed again, and Gram joined in.

"Yes, Frank sometimes did have good reason to regret the foolish things he did, but he always knew at the end of the day that it was better to come on home and face the music than to try to hide anything from me."

"I believe you, Missus Harris. Listen, I need to get going. I'm going to run over to the PR office now and work on that press release and see what we can do to help you out, okay?"

"That sounds fine, George. You have a good time meeting

with your friend from Charlotte, and please give us a quick call to let us know, one way or another, what he says, won't you?"

"I surely will, Missus Harris. Oh! There's one more thing I needed to talk to you about. I'm going to send somebody over with some papers for you to sign, certifying that you agreed to let me borrow this newspaper. It's a standard requirement with high-value artifacts such as this. When I spoke to the legal office this morning, they said that it's likely that these pages are worth as much as a million dollars, or even more."

Both Katie and Gram sat, stunned. Gram was the first to regain the power of speech. "George, did you just say 'one million dollars?'"

"Yes, Missus Harris, I did. I told you that those other documents that we looked at last night were pretty valuable, but this one is in a whole other league. I'd consider it to be in the same realm as the copy of the Jefferson Declaration of Independence that went for something like seven or eight million a few years ago, but that's just me and my bias."

He chuckled and added, "I'm torn, Missus Harris. I'd like it to be worth lots and lots, so that you can stay in your home and all of that, but I'd also like it to not be so expensive that it passes out of the university's hands. Of course, the important thing as a researcher is just that the thing exists... but I also like holding it in my own two hands as much as anyone might."

"I understand that, George. My, my... well, keep me posted, all right?"

"Sure thing, Missus Harris—I'll call you this afternoon. Bye now."

Gram hung up the phone, and Katie leaped to her feet,

grinning. "Gram, you don't have to sell the house now! We can get you a nurse to come in and check on you! Heck, you can probably hire a full-time staff now, just to wait on you hand and foot!"

"Now, now, Katie, let's don't get ahead of ourselves here. I agree that this changes things quite a bit, but we need to maintain our sense of reality, too." Then she grinned slyly at Katie and said, "Could you find me the number for the trash hauler company? I think that maybe we should cancel today's delivery of the Dumpster... we can always have them bring it another day."

Katie grinned back at her and went to find the telephone book.

# *Chapter* 10

The warm early-autumn sun slanted across the tobacco fields and lit up the trees marching up the ridge. Justin and Terrance made their way up to a freshly constructed pen, where four of the dozen lambs purchased that spring milled uneasily. Each man carried an oversized scissors-like tool, and neither looked particularly excited about the task at hand.

As part of his agreement with Gauthier for the sale of the flock, he would get three dressed lambs from Justin this fall, and Justin had decided to have one for his family, as well, though he did not intend to explain the origin of the meat to his son.

Since these four were destined for slaughter, Justin thought that it would be worthwhile for him and Terrance to try their hands at shearing with these lambs, rather than waiting until spring to have their first go at the skill, new to both men.

As they neared the pen, Justin said, "I do believe that I'll ask you to go first. After all, you spent more time at Mister Gauthier's learning how to do it than I did."

Terrance grunted, and then said good-naturedly, "But you are the master of the farm, so shouldn't you be the one to show the way?"

"Mister Gauthier said that you were a natural talent with the lambs, and I think I would do well to observe your good example."

Terrance held up his hands in a show of mock surrender. "Very well, Mister Justin. But bear in mind that I've only ever watched Mister Gauthier."

"Oh, I have great confidence in you, Terrance. Lead on!"

The negro shook his head in resignation and approached the pen. He got off to a good enough start, quickly culling out the lamb he had chosen and getting it onto the shearing blanket. He flipped it over and placed it into the position where, he had been taught, sheep become mysteriously complacent and still.

This particular lamb had apparently not learned this lesson, as it kicked and struggled for several minutes while Terrance tried to hold it still long enough to start the shearing process. When the lamb got the better of the negro and slipped out of his arms, Terrance found himself knocked backwards onto his hind end.

Charitably, Justin did not guffaw aloud, but concealed his laughter behind a hand raised to his mouth. Terrance merely looked irritated and went after the lamb, which was now grazing peacefully among the stumps in the lower field.

Catching the lamb was not as simple a matter this time around. Terrance edged up behind the beast, which watched him out of the corner of its eye, tail twitching nervously. At a distance of perhaps two or three strides, Terrance launched himself into a full run, arms outstretched to capture the lamb.

The lamb, seemingly calm, sidestepped Terrance, and the man tripped over a root, sending his arms and legs windmilling wildly as he attempted to regain his balance. By the time he rose from the dirt, covered in grass and soil, Justin had managed to suppress his outright laughter, but still had his hand clutched over his mouth, his eyes crinkled up with mirth.

Justin called out, "Do you need any assistance, Terrance?"

"No, Mister Justin. I imagine that I can outsmart this simple animal soon enough," Terrance called back through gritted teeth. His eyes narrowed as they followed the wayward sheep.

"All right, Terrance," Justin replied, his eyes still alight with amusement.

Terrance shifted tactics now, taking advantage of the fenced corner where the sheep pen butted against the side of the tobacco shed to herd the lamb into the trap. Within a minute, he had the lamb, still struggling, in his arms as he stalked back to the shearing blanket.

Whether the position was somehow different this time, or the lamb just tired enough to not feel like fighting further, when Terrance flipped it over onto its back this time, it behaved exactly as advertised, lying quietly while Terrance sized up where he'd need to start his shearing.

He had the lamb on its back, the animal's head against his thighs, and he bent double over the creature to begin shearing along its belly. Continuing the shearing up one front leg and then the other, Terrance then began clipping along the front of the leg, and up to the lamb's head.

As strip after strip of wool fell away from the animal, Justin watched closely, actually glad now that he had insisted that Terrance take the first crack at this. There was no substitute for actual experience in shearing, and there weren't enough flocks in the district to justify a full-time shearer coming here to practice his trade.

Elizabeth had assured him that she could make good use of any wool they could give her, so the better their initial efforts were, the more useful the product would be to her purposes. Along with the shears, Justin had purchased carders and a hand spindle at her specification. Justin knew that she yearned for a proper spinning wheel, but with the open warfare now upon the Colonies, such investments would need to wait for a more propitious time.

Justin had heard in the village that the British had lost one fort along the Savannah River but had regained another not far from the first. He felt sharply divided loyalties warring within himself. On the one hand, he agreed with a lot of what Jeremiah had to say about the overall high level freedom of that the British crown permitted its subjects.

On the other hand, it seemed as though the Parliament was arbitrarily starting to take away some of the most important rights granted to Englishmen everywhere else, and with no real justification, other than that they had the naked power to do so.

Shaking off his ruminations, Justin was pleased to see that Terrance had nearly finished with the first lamb. After a few more minutes of careful clipping, the negro turned the lamb over, set it on its legs, and gave it a smack to send it on its way.

He grinned up at Justin as he bundled up the wool. "Your turn, Mister Justin."

Justin sighed to himself as Terrance finished clearing the shearing blanket. Selecting the lamb he planned to work on, he hauled it over to the shearing blanket and wrestled it into position. Unlike Terrance's lamb, this one did settle right down, and Justin picked up his shears to start clipping it.

The first cuts were somewhat difficult, as Justin worked his way through the matted dirt and grass on the animal's underside. Once he got through that layer, though, he found that the shears made short work of the wool close to the lamb's skin.

Justin worked slowly and methodically, clearing away the dirty parts of the lamb's wool first, and then moving on to the soft, clean areas on the animal's shoulders, flanks and back. The sharp smell of lanolin combined with the field smell from the lamb's underside, but Justin found that he didn't mind it.

Just as he was getting into a good rhythm and had started on the lamb's other flank, the animal suddenly bleated and started struggling. Justin pulled the shears away, for fear of stabbing the lamb on the sharpened tips of the blades, and was horrified to see that it was bleeding profusely from a nick where the shears had caught a fold of skin.

He looked up at Terrance, who shook his head with a sympathetic expression on his face. "It happens, Mister Justin. Remember that Mister Gauthier told us that they heal up in no time, and it doesn't cause them that much upset. It'll be fine."

Justin sighed and bent over the lamb again, which was, indeed, already significantly calmed down. He completed the shearing without further incident, and sent the lamb on its way. The bleeding had already stopped, and the animal didn't seem any the worse for the wear.

He gathered up and tied the fleece, setting it aside as he and Terrance each retrieved their second lambs. Working side-by-side, they both made relatively quick work of the task their second time through. As they gathered up their fleeces, Justin got a good look at the freshly-shorn lambs for the first time and laughed aloud.

The lambs stood close together with the rest of the flock, their bearing suggesting that they felt embarrassed at their appearance. Their coats had obviously been shorn by amateurs, and were uneven and even patchy in a couple of places. Justin chortled to the negro, "Oh, those poor things! What have we done to them?"

Terrance turned and looked where Justin was pointing, and started chuckling himself. "I guess we'll just do better next time, Mister Justin. They do look pretty silly, though."

Timothy met them at the door to the house and was quite excited about the fleeces but even more amused at the shorn sheep cavorting together now in the field. He and Katherine ran out, shrieking with joy, to play with the sheep.

Justin hauled three of the bundled fleeces up into the loft and set the fourth in a tub full of water in Elizabeth's sewing corner, where she had told him she wanted it. She had explained to him that she would leave it there for a number of days for its natural cleansing process to take effect.

"Though," she had said, "I do wish that we could let it work out-of-doors, as it is not the most pleasant-smelling thing in the world."

Justin sat at the table, his back aching from the extended time doubled over the two lambs. "I hope the wool is of good quality," he said to her.

"Time will tell," she said, smiling. "How did it go?"

"Well, I nicked one of them a bit, and one of them thought it could outsmart Terrance here, but he showed it who was boss in the end, eh?"

Terrance smiled as he reached around and kneaded the muscles of his lower back. "There's no sheep alive can outsmart me," he said with a grin.

The three of them chuckled together as the children came back inside, laughing and excited to describe the funny-looking lambs they had been playing with.

Justin drew a deep breath, happy to see Katherine fully recovered from her encounter with the rattlesnake earlier that summer. He looked at Terrance, who was watching the children with a cheerful smile on his face, and was thankful all over again for the chance that had brought the negro into his household.

A few days after the snake incident, Justin had finally brought himself to tell the slave about his agreement with Jeremiah. Terrance had accepted the news of his sale to Justin with equanimity, saying nothing further than, "I do like working tobacco better than indigo."

When Terrance didn't see him watching, though, Justin thought that he saw a certain wistfulness in the negro's expression for many weeks after. He wondered at that, but could not think of a way to ask the negro what was troubling him, and eventually dismissed it. Terrance seemed happy and at ease with Justin's family, and Elizabeth and the children appreciated having him around.

As for himself, Justin continued to find things that Terrance simply knew how to do that were highly valuable around the farm, and his strong and reliable labor at more mundane jobs continued to impress Justin and reinforce in his mind that he had made the correct decision.

# Chapter II

While they waited to hear back from George, Katie called her mother.

"Hi, Mum," she began.

"Hello, Katie. How are things going with Gram's house?"

"We're making good progress, but something interesting has come up." Katie struggled to keep her voice even. "What can you tell me about Justin Harris?"

"Justin Harris? Oh, you mean on the family tree? Just a moment, let me go get that."

"Sure thing, Mum."

After a minute, Katie could hear background noises of papers rustling and her mother picked up the phone again. "All right, Justin, you said?"

"Yes," Katie confirmed.

"All right, I don't have a whole lot on him. The family Bible showed that he was born in 1747, died in 1801, married to Elizabeth Laurens, who was born in 1749 and died in 1815. Actually, their daughter Katherine is who you're named after—I remember Grandpa being tickled that we'd gone into his family names for our last child."

Katie replied, "Great, thanks! I can probably fill in some more details on Justin and Elizabeth for you, as well as some others, though I haven't gone through everything yet. We found a whole chest full of old papers here, some of which go all the way back to the Revolution."

Katie's mother exclaimed, "Oh, my, how exciting! What did you find on Justin and Elizabeth, exactly?"

"So far, it appears that Justin fought under a Colonel Thompson in the Revolution, and was decorated for his role. Also, it's possible that he was the original owner of Gram's house, starting back in 1760-something?"

"Oh, that's wonderful information! Really helps you get a sense of the family, you know?"

"It sure does, Mum. Also, the chest has Elizabeth's name on it on a brass plaque, which is very interesting. But, Mum, there was something else in those papers, too."

"Oh?" Her mother's voice had a note of alarm in it. "Like what?"

"Nothing bad, Mum... in fact, something possibly very good for Gram. Have you ever heard of the Mecklenburg Declaration of Independence?"

"No, I can't say that I have, Katie. What does this have to do with old family papers?"

"It all ties in, let me just explain. I guess that some guys in Mecklenberg County, up in North Carolina, jumped the gun a little bit on the whole business of breaking away from England and being their own country. They wrote a Declaration more than a year before the one for the whole country was passed."

"Huh. I had never heard about this before. Fascinating!"

"You might not have heard about it, because it was considered to be a myth, I guess debunked by Jefferson himself. In any case, one of the problems with it was that nobody had a copy of the thing—it was lost in a fire after the Revolution."

"That does sound sort of fishy to me, I'll admit. How did this thing come to light?"

"From what I could learn, there was a newspaper article in like 1820 or so, where someone who had been at the Mecklenberg meeting had written it down from memory after the fire."

"No wonder it was considered mythical, then."

"Right. Well, it's not mythical, Mum. We found a newspaper that published it a few weeks after it was passed, right here in Gram's attic!"

"Good heavens! Really?"

"Yeah! They're checking it out right now, but if it turns out to be the real thing, it'll re-write at least part of the history of the American Revolution. One of Grandpa's old friends works at the university, and he's got an expert coming down from Charlotte to look it over. And here's the best part, Mum—if it's real, it's worth a lot of money."

"What does that mean, exactly? How much is 'a lot?'"

"Millions, Mum. Enough that Gram can stay in the house, and not have to sell it off. Mum, I had no idea that this place had been in the family for almost two hundred and fifty years! I really hope that this isn't just a horrible mistake, because I've realized that I would love to stay here after I finish my residency. This is a really nice town, and I'm sure I could do well here."

"But what about Denver, Katie? Didn't you have a friend out there?"

"Oh, Mum, Johnny turned out to be a loser, and I just hadn't figured out what I wanted to do instead. Now I have a pretty good idea, and I just want it to all work out, you know?"

"I guess I can see that... gracious. Keep me posted, and give Gram my love, will you?"

"Sure thing, Mum. Let Pop know all about it, too, would you? I'm sure Gram would love to hear from him, too."

"Okay, dear, I'll send him an email later tonight. Bye-bye."

"Bye, Mum."

Katie sat back after putting the phone back on its charger and thought. She hadn't really formulated any particular plan of what to do with the new situation until she talked it through with her mother, but the more she thought about it, the more she liked it.

General practitioners were pretty much in high demand everywhere, and she had always had a soft spot in her heart for Gram's home town. The idea of maybe even living here with Gram just filled her heart with joy, and she decided that she'd broach the subject with her once they knew more about the documents and Gram's plans.

The call came in the early afternoon, a couple of hours after a messenger had brought the paperwork over to record the loan of certain potentially valuable artifacts to the Department of History at the University. George's voice on the phone sounded of scarcely contained joy. "Missus Harris?"

Gram answered, "Yes?"

"According to Doctor Marshall, he is ninety-five percent certain that this document is genuine. The paper is right, the printing method matches, the ink appears to be right, and, more important, the content rings authentic to his eyes."

"Glory be," Gram whispered, for once at a complete loss

for words. She recovered after a moment, and asked, "So, the press will be notified this afternoon?"

"Yes, Missus Harris. The release is being finalized at this end now, and I'll have a copy of it messengered over to your house for your approval before we send it out. I've got someone from the public relations office who will come over to assist you with any press contacts this evening, okay?"

"Yes, that sounds good, George, thank you."

"What she's told me—her name, by the way, is Heidi McIntosh—is that you can expect maybe a day or two of a lot of media attention, maybe with television crews and all of that out on your street, wanting interviews and so on."

"Oh, dear. Well, I suppose I can give interviews. I'll have to ask Katie to help me tidy up the living room and move the boxes she had put down here, but that won't take long."

"Exactly. After that, there will be a bus crash or a windsurfing squirrel or something, and they'll mostly dash off in pursuit of the next story, but there will probably be a few magazines and so on who will have questions for you over the next few months. Those people will be less interested in the sensational story, and will have more questions that Bill or I will be able to handle."

"Okay, I understand that. I'm sorry, Bill is...?"

"Oh, sorry—Bill Alexander, my colleague who came down from Charlotte this morning. He's actually descended from a bunch of the signers of the Mecklenberg Declaration, so he's been interested in this particular issue of the *Mercury* for a very, very long time."

"I can imagine! Okay, is there anything else I need to know?"

"Well, I'm working under the assumption that you are planning to sell this document?"

"George, I have thought about that a lot, and I've concluded that I have no possible use for the thing myself, and much as I would love to donate it to the University, it would make my life a whole lot simpler if I could sell it and make enough money to avoid having to sell the house."

"I understand entirely, Missus Harris, and I thank you kindly for giving the University at least some thought in your decision-making process. The reason that I asked, though, is just to let you know that the other media frenzy Heidi asked me to give you a heads-up on would happen when the document sells, if it goes for anything like what I personally think it's worth." He paused for a moment.

"That sort of story is exactly what people like to see on the news, you know? They like to think that there might be something like that up in their own attic, that they could strike it rich. So, the television stations will probably want to talk to you all over again then... just so you know."

"Well, George, if it comes to that, I may be able to hire Heidi to do some free-lance work for me, right?" Gram chuckled.

George laughed along with her and replied, "I suppose that could be true, Missus Harris, we'll see. Okay, did you have any other questions? I'm supposed to be meeting with the Dean in a couple of minutes, but I wanted to make sure that you were fully informed first."

"No, I think that's everything I needed to know right now. When should I expect the messenger?"

"Within an hour, I expect, Missus Harris. If you don't see

any changes you need us to make, could you just call me on my mobile and let me know, so that we can get it on the wire right away?"

"Certainly, George. Thanks for having them run it by me."

"It's the least I can do, Missus Harris. Okay, then, I'll talk to you in a little while."

"In a little while, George. Good-bye."

Gram hung up the phone and turned to Katie, who was nearly jumping up and down with joy at the news. "Well, Katie, let's get this place in shape for the circus, shall we?"

# Chapter 12

"Well, Terrance, that went better than last fall, didn't it?" Justin was sweaty, covered in mud and bits of airborne wool, as well as a few spots of blood from a nicked lamb, but there were seven neatly tied fleeces arrayed along the tobacco shed, and the yearling lambs were running about in the field, getting accustomed to their lighter coats.

"Yes, sir, Mister Justin, we have done well." Terrance looked hardly better than Justin, though the mud was not as evident on his rougher, more stained clothing.

Justin turned to Harold Gauthier, who had come over to give advice. "I thank you, Harold, for your time and good counsel. I appreciate, too, your assistance in bringing these fleeces to market."

Gauthier shifted the jackstraw dangling from his mouth before replying. "You are most welcome, neighbor. You made a shrewd investment in these sheep, I daresay. What with the war getting ever more heated, demand for wool, and the price it will fetch, have both gone up a great deal since last spring."

"I am most gratified to hear that, in truth, since my tobacco harvest is getting to be harder to bring to market these days." Justin had been glad to ship four hogsheads to Jeremiah, and had quickly received the bill of sale for Terrance in return. The harvest had been good, yielding nearly a full fifth hogshead, but prices had been disappointing, so the extra income from the wool was very welcome indeed.

"I'm glad we got nine new lambs, although the birthing was an interesting experience! I've dealt with hogs once before, but Terrance here has attended not only hogs, but cattle as well. Sheep, of course, are a little different from either of those, but with his help, we got through it."

Justin's previous experience with hogs had ended sadly—the sow they had started with in their first year on the farm had thrown one litter, and then had gotten into something in the forest that had sickened and killed her in a matter of hours. The piglets had been too young to wean, and so Justin had had to slaughter them all at once, and the experience had left him perfectly willing to barter for pork ever since. Turkeys were a lot easier to manage, in his opinion.

"What news of the war, Harold? I've heard a lot throughout the winter about the British engaging American troops in New England, and I know that they've taken some forts around here, as well."

The older man considered for a few moments, and then answered, "Justin, let me put it this way. I would not plan on visiting Charles Town while the British are about. They've been arming the savages, as you know, and quite a few travelers have failed to reach their destinations. Even worse, I've heard it said that if the British themselves find an able-bodied man, they are liable to impress him directly into the Royal Navy, with not so much as a fare-thee-well to his family."

"I've heard the same, and I had already decided that traveling under these conditions was a bad idea. Have you heard anything more about the naval battle at Charles Town harbor?"

"Yes, an entire artillery company of Pennsylvanians, coming to reinforce the Continental Army's positions around Charles Town, was taken captive. Even worse, their powder and supplies went to the British forces instead of the American."

Gauthier chewed some more on his straw, and then seemed to reach a decision. "Young Mister Harris, some of us have been talking about organizing patrols, to safeguard the farms in the district. Your name has come up in those discussions, as we worry about you and your family out so far from the village. What would you think about being a part of that effort?"

Justin considered it for a long moment. He knew that joining even an informal militia of this nature would be considered an act of treason against the Crown. On the other hand, the Crown's soldiers were failing to observe the customary niceties in quartering with civilians and were often behaving more like marauding invaders.

"Harold, I will need to ponder on that for a while, if it's all right with you. I understand the need for the patrol... but I'm still hoping for the British commanders to rein in their men. Perhaps I am being naïve, but one of the marks of a civilized military is their good conduct regardless of circumstance."

Gauthier replied, "Justin, let me speak plainly to you. You know Phillip Prescott and his wife Hannah, over on the far side of town?"

"Yes, fine people, lovely family. They have wonderful children, and a well-run farm. In fact, Phillip loaned me an extra axe when I brought Terrance on, and I'm grateful to you for reminding me that I need to return it now."

"Justin, last week, they were visited by the British. Their slaves were taken and shipped back to Georgia, from what Phillip has said ... I'm sorry to say that Hannah and eldest daughter were... abused by the troops."

Justin blinked hard at this news. It was one of his worst nightmares, visited upon a friend, an unsuspecting farmer who, like himself, had wanted to just stay clear of controversy and tend to his own business. Justin thought about the broadside his cousin had given to him, a paper whose words he had read over many times since returning with it. After another moment's thought and a deep breath, he said, "Harold, you have me convinced. How are we planning to organize?"

For years afterward, he would remember that moment, when a sudden cold sweat trickled down his forehead, making him forget the aches and filth of the day's work, as he turned away from his former King and committed himself to the cause of independency from Britain.

# Chapter 13

The last of the satellite vans had lowered their telescoping booms and packed up their cargoes of painted reporters and bored cameramen. The flowerbeds had been abused with cables and even the occasional misstep by a technician. Gram's iced tea supply was depleted, and both she and Katie sat, exhausted, in the living room.

The phone rang, and Katie wearily sat up to answer it. "Can you call back tomorrow, please?" she asked mechanically.

"Well, I guess I can, if you insist, but I was hoping to speak to my mother," came the cheerful voice.

"Pop! Wow, it's so good to hear from you! What time is it there?"

Gram perked up at this and sat forward, listening now, her eyes alight.

"Oh, it's about five in the morning, I think. I just got up and got your Mum's email and thought I'd call. It all sounds very exciting! Tell me, was this in the trunk that had the nameplate on it, or the one that Grandpa kept the guns locked up in?"

"Is that what's in there? Do you know where the key is?"

"No, he never told me, but I found it unlocked one time after he'd been out after a rabbit in the garden. Boy, did he ever tan my hide for that!" He chuckled at the memory.

"Is that all that's in there?"

"I didn't dig around in there much, but that's all I remember seeing. Of course, I was probably all of eleven or twelve years old, so I wasn't looking at anything else, I'm sure. That other trunk was boring, boring—all clothing and papers that I was afraid to mess up, lest Grandpa get out the strap. He always yelled at me for going up into the attic and looking through the things. So, all of the exciting stuff was in that chest, then, huh?"

"Sure was, Pop. We've sent most of it over to the University for the time being, but I guess Gram's going to have to figure out what she wants to sell and how to go about it. George Branton is going to help her out, though."

"Oh, yeah, George! My gosh, I haven't talked to him in a dog's age! He must be about fit to be tied with all of this, huh?"

"Oh, yeah, you should have seen him shaking when we found just the less important stuff. I seriously thought he was having a heart attack when he saw the newspaper."

"Boy, I'll bet. When you talk to him, give him my congratulations on the find, and let him know I'm thinking about him."

"Sure thing, Pop."

"Can I talk to Gram now?"

"You bet, just a sec."

Katie grinned and handed the phone over to Gram.

"Joe, how nice to hear from you! Are you staying safe over there?" Katie couldn't make out her Pop's words, but could hear the reassuring tone, and could imagine him painting a picture of just an ordinary place of business. True, the insurgency had tapered down, his contributions were very important and he was making enough money to allow him retire early when he got back home, if he wanted to. Still, Katie prayed every night for his safe return and worried about him whenever she let herself think about it.

"Yes, it's a great comfort to think that I can keep the house and stay here. I know that's what your father wanted, but, bless his heart, he expected to have another ten or twenty years to see to it, and we all know that that didn't happen."

Pop replied briefly, and Gram continued, "Well, in any case, I guess he did manage to provide for me, after all, with his packrat ways, and his grandpa's, and probably *his* grandfather's before him. You will never believe what Katie found up there." Gram told her son about the boxes of kitchen junk drawer contents, and Katie could hear Pop's roar of laughter clearly from across the room.

"Stubborn, stubborn man, your father was, Joe, but I guess you take after him that way, don't you?"

Pop answered her, his voice quieter again, and Gram nodded. "Yes, I know you think you're keeping yourself safe, Joe, but I read the papers and watch the news." Pop interrupted her, and Gram listened, frowning.

"Well, if you say so... Okay... All right, well thanks so much for calling. It's good to hear your voice again, and I'm glad to share such good news... Thanks, I'll pray for you, too. Bye-bye."

Gram lowered the phone away from her ear and slowly pressed the disconnect key. "Your father," she shook her head sadly to Katie, "will be the death of me, I swear. Oh, well. It *was* good to hear from him, and I'm glad he's not worrying about me going to the nursing home anymore."

Gram noted the look of surprised amusement on Katie's face. "Oh yes, I know it was a nursing home, where I would go and watch my friends and companions drop dead around me, until the day that it was my turn to roll out the door under a sheet. I just didn't see what other option I had, until now."

Katie saw that Gram's eyes were bright with unshed tears. "Katie, you were always such a joy on your visits here, and I don't know that anyone else would have found those papers. You saved me from that fate, and I don't have any words to thank you enough."

"Oh, Gram," said Katie, rising to kneel beside her grandmother's chair, so that she could embrace the older woman. "I'm just so glad they were there to be found. I was so scared for you going to that place, no matter how nice it sounded."

"I know, Katydid, I could tell that you were unhappy. But there really wasn't any other way that I could see." Gram sighed deeply and smiled. "But now, thanks to your care in helping me do something you hated to see me do, there is another way."

"I'm really glad to have helped, Gram. And I'm glad, too, that we'll still get to spend our summers together here. For a couple more years, at least, until I start my residency," she laughed. "But after that, well, I was sort of thinking that it might be nice if I could start my practice here, so that I can be close by."

Gram looked startled, and then began crying quietly. "Katie, child, I can think of nothing that would make me happier than to have you here in town. For that matter, I don't need to rattle around in this big house by myself—there's plenty of room for you here, if you'd like that."

"Oh, Gram, I'd love that," Katie replied enthusiastically. "It would be like spending summer with you all year around," she said, grinning.

"Well, I would probably make you do more chores than

you did during your summers," Gram said, smiling back. "After all, look at how well this weekend of hard labor has worked out!"

They laughed together, the tears drying quickly on dimpled and wrinkled cheeks alike.

# Chapter 14

Justin's mare picked her way down the slope through the undergrowth, her footing steady despite the incline. His musket was a comfortable weight over his shoulder, and he was relatively relaxed. There were no reports of British troops in the district recently, but all of the members of the village's "Committee of Safety" were keenly aware of the depredations that had been visited upon their neighbor.

Through the other men in the group, Justin learned the lurid details of Prescott's torment, in stories that hardened his heart against any Redcoats that might be skulking around the district. "They caught him unawares, working the fields with his negroes," a grizzled plantation owner had told him.

"The soldiers secured the house first. They laughed as they bound Hannah and the children, and then went looking for Phillip. Unarmed, faced with five *brave* Redcoats, all pointing muskets and bayonets at his belly, he had no way to resist the bastards." The man spat, emphasizing his disgust with the British troops.

As Justin shook his head in anger, another man picked up the story. "They bound him and his negroes hand and foot, and then proceeded to plunder everything that wasn't nailed down. A couple of the soldiers decided to have their way with his wife first, and then his daughter, while Phillip watched. I don't know about him, but I think I would have gone mad, watching that."

"I think he did, a little bit," said a third man, an overseer at a large plantation near Prescott's. "Ain't seen him smile even once since then, and I surely wouldn't want to be a British soldier within range of his rifle. Don't think you'd have time to make peace with your Maker afore you met him in person, you know?"

The other men had nodded grimly, and they seemed to share the sentiment. Hannah and Molly Prescott were in the care of the wife of the plantation owner whose overseer had spoken, but there was no way to heal the hurts done to the Prescott family by the British. The common sentiment seemed to be that the only relief would be through revenge.

Vengeance for a violence done to an honest friend was a far greater motivation than any theoretical question of parliaments or kings, and all of the men of the Committee loudly hoped—and quietly feared—that they would be the ones to deliver a taste of that vengeance.

These thoughts were heavy in Justin's head as he came onto a clearing in the wood. The breeze shifted, and he smelled a campfire, rich with the aroma of a stew bubbling over it. Immediately, he stopped his mare and dismounted, knowing from experience that she would stay put.

Creeping through the trees, his every sense alert, Justin quickly spotted the encampment. Eight men and horses, with an extra two pack horses, were picketed along the south edge of the meadow. They seemed at ease, their uniforms in casual condition, rather than the close-ordered spotlessness that was usual for Redcoats.

He could hear their laughter now, as they shared supper and passed around a bottle. Silently, he cursed himself for not having equipped himself with a proper rifle. He knew he could only get one shot off before having to flee the rest of the troops.

Priming his weapon carefully and quietly behind a tree, just a few dozen yards from the campfire, he thought about what he was preparing to do. To quiet his qualms about firing on another human being, he reminded himself that these laughing men might well be the same ones who had replaced the ready smile of Phillip Prescott with the haunted look of a man who has seen the unthinkable.

With his musket ready to fire, Justin took a position where he could observe the British. He noted that the men showed deference to one of their number, handing the bottle over to the ruddy-cheeked man without question when he held out his hand for it. His target picked, Justin shouldered the musket and took aim, his heart hammering against his ribcage.

He breathed deeply, taking in the smell of the warm early summer air, mingled with the smoke from the fire. A bird sang out above him, and he exhaled, his finger tightening over the trigger. He didn't even hear the roar of the musket as it fired, but rather the shouts of the man's companions as he fell heavily to the ground, groaning as his shirt was stained with a fresh scarlet brighter than the jacket over it.

As if the world were standing still around him, Justin ran to his mare and leaped into the saddle, spurring her back up the slope. He heard shots fired behind him, but no telltale whir of balls in close proximity. Within a few minutes, he was over the other side of the hill, making for the safety of the next ridge. No pursuit sounded behind him, and eventually, he slowed his mare to a walk.

Now that the danger was past, he found himself quaking in his saddle, his hands shaking uncontrollably on the reins. He noted that his musket was back over his shoulder, though he had no memory of re-slinging it.

His clearest memory was of the look of utter shock on the man's ruddy face as the ball struck his shoulder. It was an instant that would revisit Justin in his dreams for years to come, and which would never truly leave him for the rest of his days.

The afternoon sun shone through the trees, its rays illuminating a mossy boulder here, a fallen tree there, the web of an ambitious spider to one side of the horse path. Justin knew that the man he'd shot would no more be witness to the wonder of Creation, and he felt a heavy responsibility to carry the weight of his victim's lost experience in his own appreciation for the world around him.

When he got back to the village, Harold Gauthier was there, preparing for his patrol. The look on Justin's face told him most of what he needed to know.

"Justin, you look a fright, and you're back before I expected you. You found something on your patrol?"

"I... I killed a man, Harold. He was a redcoat... I shot him down in cold blood, and I fled back to here." Justin was beyond being able to even feel any shame at the tears that poured out in a torrent along with the words.

"Steady there, Justin. Let's go inside, and you can tell me about it, all right?"

Justin followed the older man into the village tavern, which was close at hand, and the two sat at a table in the quietest corner of the room. Gauthier raised to fingers to the innkeeper, who nodded and silently brought over two small pewter cups of a potent, brown fluid.

"Drink this." Gauthier pushed one of the cups toward Justin, who mechanically poured it past his dry lips and then gasped as the burn of the roughly-distilled rum hit his throat.

Speaking in a low tone, Gauthier leaned forward and fixed Justin with an intense gaze. "Now, tell me, Justin. Was the man you shot alone?" Justin shook his head, his eyes still streaming.

"If you had shown yourself, what would have happened?"

Justin, finding his voice again, replied in a monotone, "I likely would have been impressed into the Royal Navy—or worse."

"And, if you had ridden away, without doing anything, what would have happened?"

"I don't know."

"Justin, you have seen Prescott. Now tell me, what would have happened, had you let those men move freely through our district?"

Justin thought for a long moment, then looked Gauthier steadily in the eye and spoke quietly and firmly. "I know what would have happened, Harold. I knew the moment I saw them what they were here for. Do you think that I would have fired if I didn't know? Do you think that I would have taken the life of a man who once dandled on his mother's knee, whose sweetheart pines for him in England, whose fellow soldiers are mourning him even as we speak? I knew, Harold, and that's why I fired my weapon. I also know that the wrath of those soldiers who are digging his grave now may be awful to witness, and that I *will* be witness to it. I know, Harold."

Gauthier nodded. "I was certain that you did, Justin. Now you are certain, too. You did the right thing, and you need to know that, as well. You had a choice; you could have hoped that what befell somebody else's hearth and home last time would again spare your own. You could have left that band to commit whatever acts of savagery they were sent hither to perform and fled with your family to a safer place."

The older man took Justin's chin in his hand and looked him in the eye. "But you didn't. You stood today for the defense of not just your own wife and children, but for the defense of your nation. Today, you became an American." He released Justin, who closed his eyes for a long moment, absorbing the man's words.

In a whisper, he said, "I *am* an American. I am no longer a subject of the British Crown. I have committed an act of rebellion and treason against the King who I once held as my sovereign. I am an American."

"Yes, Justin. You are, and will be to the end of your days. You have been for a long time, and now you know it." Gauthier squared his shoulders and sat upright, then said, a little louder, but still quietly enough that the innkeeper and a traveler sitting at the front of the room could not hear, "So. What will you do now?"

"What do you mean?"

"Will you return to your farm, and play no more at war... until it comes to your doorstep? Will you go on being a patrolman in the Committee of Safety?"

Once again, Gauthier fixed Justin within the focus of his strong personality. "Or will you move to be certain that your act of bravery today for the cause of the American nation shall not be in vain?"

Justin looked at the other man questioningly. "How do you mean, Harold?"

"Colonel Thompson is raising a company of riflemen, Justin,

to go to Charles Town and defend it from the British, should they attempt to take it by sea. No," he raised his hand as Justin started to speak, "I know you have no rifle, but I am sure that you are a steady shot, else you could not have felled your target today. I can find a rifle for you, if it's needed."

"But my wife, my children, my farm—"

"The men of the Committee will see to the safety of your family, Justin, just as we have seen to Prescott's since we formed up. As for your farm, you have a good negro there, and he can carry on in your absence, although you will probably have to cut back your crop for the duration. But tell me, Justin, what is more important to you: a couple of hogsheads of tobacco, or the freedom to raise it unmolested?"

Justin took a deep breath, and then nodded, convinced. Quietly, he replied, "All right. What need I do?"

"Wait here; I'll be back in a few minutes. Drink this." Gauthier shoved the other cup across the table, and Justin nodded and drank it, his face slowly flushing red as his throat burned again, but maintaining his composure this time.

# Chapter 15

K atie sat in the darkness of her room, the light of her small television reflecting from her face, the sound turned low, so as not to disturb Gram's sleep. The evening news still carried the jarring image in the background of the house Katie knew so well, with Gram talking to yet another plastic surgery beneficiary on her sweeping driveway.

The commentary from the anchor, though, got Katie's attention. "We talked to one expert who is not convinced that this alleged newspaper is authentic. For more on this story, let's turn to Jeff Talmage, in Roanoke. Jeff?"

"Yes, Lee, earlier today, we spoke with Professor Lawrence Schulmann, who is a leading expert on forgeries of Revolution-era documents."

Katie gasped and almost missed what the balding man with small eyes and a classic combover was saying into the microphone the reporter shoved into his face. His nasal voice droned, "Mister Talmage, we see a rash of these claims nearly every summer, as people start to think about the Revolution for a few days, if even that. Sadly, some people's thoughts turn to ways in which they can profit from the thirst for real history that still burns in the hearts of a few passionate, if misguided collectors out there."

Talmage pulled the microphone back as the academic took a breath, obviously ready to continue at length. "But, Professor

Schulmann, have you seen this document, or learned anything that convinces you that this is what's happening in this case?"

Given the opportunity to speak again, the mousy little man started in again. "Well, Mister Talmage, it frankly strains credulity to ask us to believe that this widow could be completely unaware of the contents of an unlocked chest in the attic of the house where her husband's family had allegedly resided for over a hundred years. I am sad to say that it is apparent to me that what we're dealing with here is a case of a college student's prank on the part of this poor woman's granddaughter, based on superficial research on the Internet. She is, obviously, hoping to profit by her actions, and I am only glad to be of service to the collectors' community in ensuring that this hoax not go undetected."

Katie's jaw dropped at this comment, but Professor Schulmann wasn't finished yet. "However, she is, sadly, clearly ignorant of is the history of hoaxes and frauds with this particular item. I know from my research and extensive writing on the period that the *Cape Fear Mercury*, which she purports to having 'discovered' in her grandmother's attic, had ceased publication before the date of the issue in question."

Katie gasped aloud this time, her hands flying to her mouth. The professor droned on, "This was the single fact that most undermined the last attempt to manufacture a proof of the so-called Mecklenburg Declaration, which, perhaps not coincidentally, revolved around another forged issue of this same newspaper."

The reporter gamely tried to haul Schulmann back to his original question. "But, Professor, have you actually seen this purported document?"

Shulmann airily waved a hand. "No, nor do I expect to

be granted access to it. After all, my esteemed colleagues"—he placed a particular stress on these words—"who rushed news of their 'discovery' to the media, rather than waiting for publication of a properly peer-reviewed article in the appropriate professional historians' journals, well, let's just say that they don't have anything in particular to gain from letting someone who could expose exactly how they were duped see the purported documents. However, once their formulaic angry *ad hominem* denunciations of me and my work have been issued, the community of Revolution-era historians will, I am confident, find that they have little choice but to come to a position of agreement with me."

"Thank you, Professor." The reporter turned away from Shulmann, whose mouth was already open to add another comment. "So, Lee, there you have it. We have either the most sensational find in decades of colonial research, or a clever ruse undertaken for the sake of a few dollars. This is Jeff Talmage, and I'll be reporting on the latest developments in this rapidly-evolving story."

Katie was livid as she viciously punched the power button on the remote. She sat in the darkness for a few minutes, fuming. Worse, after a few more minutes, she began to wonder whether the historian's doubts might not have some sort of a basis in the truth. Was is possible that someone over the years had forged and then stuffed the fake documents in with other documents from the same era, for the purpose of committing a hoax, perhaps at a later date?

She knew one thing for certain, though. She would be calling George Branton the first thing in the morning. With that resolve, she rolled over and willed sleep to come, in spite of the doubts and fears that roiled in her head and disrupted her sleep all

# Chapter 16

night long.

Corporal Justin Harris, newly assigned to the defense of the Charles Town harbor, shouted above the constant din of hammers ringing against nails, "Mister Cooper! Get those timbers over there! We need to get the next section started!" Cooper turned his head toward Justin and scowled, but directed his mule toward the end of the hastily—but stoutly constructed—makeshift wall of soft palmetto logs that rose around the encampment of men from Colonel Thompson's brigade.

Cooper grumbled as he maneuvered the cart into position and untied the load, letting the stout, green timbers roll and bounce to a rest in the heavy clay of Sullivan's Island. Like the other local laborers who had been pressed into service, he was none too pleased to be given orders by Thompson's men, but all knew that the fort was absolutely essential to the defense of the harbor—and, by extension, the whole of Charles Town.

Justin led a group of men over to where the teamster's cart stood. As the load finished rumbling off of the side, the soldiers sprang into action, lifting the logs into place in a well-coordinated and practiced rhythm. The teamster leaned against the wheel of his cart. "So, you reckon that the Brits will try to close the harbor, eh?"

"Mister Cooper, it's the only thing keeping their siege of

the city from being absolute. Not only that, but they've already blockaded the Boston and Philadelphia harbors, so Charles Town is the last major sea harbor the Colonies have open." Justin nodded grimly at the choppy, slate-grey waters of the harbor. "If I were the British, I'd be doing everything in my power to shut down this harbor. I'm just surprised that they're not here already."

Justin offered the teamster his hand, which the other man shook briefly. "Mister Cooper, I do appreciate your willingness to offer your services." He looked around, and then added, confidentially, "I know that they're paying you in Colonial bank notes, but I've got some tobacco from my farm that I would be pleased to offer you as an additional token of my personal gratitude for your help. I know that the Loyalists in town have been refusing to accept the bank notes, but tobacco is good everywhere."

Cooper's eyebrows went up, and he replied, "Well, I thank you kindly, Corporal Harris." He accepted the packet that Justin offered, and caused it to disappear about his voluminous person. His eyes narrowed for a moment, and he asked, "Begging your pardon, Corporal, but are you, by chance, related to the Tory Harrises here in Charles Town?"

Justin bowed his head and grimaced. "Yes, they are my kin," he admitted. "None has had a word to say to me since hearing that I had joined up with Colonel Thompson's brigade. They have not seen, and do not believe, what the British irregulars have done in places like my district. My own neighbor, Private Prescott, was the subject of a raid earlier this year, and I cannot bear to speak of what was done to his family."

Cooper nodded, his lips pressed grimly together. "I've heard the tales, Corporal Harris, and I have no trouble believing them.

Some of those Brits regard us as somehow lesser than themselves and treat the Colonists worse than they would treat dogs."

Justin sighed. "Well, standing around talking about it isn't going to get this fort built," he said.

Cooper stood and put his foot into the stirrup. Pausing before he mounted, he said, "Best of luck to you, Corporal Harris, if my next load doesn't bring me to your detail."

"Thank you kindly, Mister Cooper. May you and your kin fare well in the days to come, as well."

As the teamster's wagon rolled bumpily out of the nascent fort, a young man ran in, a wild look in his eye. He hailed Justin. "Sir! Can you direct me to the commander of the fort?"

Justin returned his wave of greeting and replied, "What business have you with him?"

"I have an urgent message from Captain Greenfeld, sir, from Wither's Swash, up north from this position."

"Very well," said Justin, startled into action. He pointed at a tent that sat just inside the outer wall of the fort. "That tent there, beside the flagpole, is the one you want." He turned back to his work, calling over a crew to begin raising the posts for the next run of the wall, while another group began raising the earthworks behind the last run, reinforcing its soft timbers.

A few minutes later, a sergeant walked up briskly. "Corporal Harris?"

"Yes, Sergeant, that is I."

"The commander has asked me to inform all of the crew leaders that we are to redouble our efforts to complete as much of the fort as possible with the materials we have on hand now."

"What is the reason for this? The men will want to

know."

"The British fleet has been sighted, Corporal." Justin was momentarily stunned into silence. It was one thing to face a small troop of irregulars from the relative safety of the woods of his own district. To face the firepower of the British Navy, with its well-ordered officers and seamen, and their notoriously efficient gunship fusillades, well, that was something else indeed.

"Corporal Harris, your men," said the sergeant, bringing Justin back to the task at hand. "You are free to tell them; it may encourage their work." Justin shuddered inwardly, but gave no outward sign of his fears.

Justin nodded curtly to the sergeant, and then turned and assessed at a glance what could be completed and what would have to wait in hopes of future shipments of materials. He bellowed to his work detail, "Step it up, men! The British have been sighted, and it is only a matter of time now before they have us in their sights!"

He strode over to the earthworks that rose behind the wall, and grabbed a shovel, bending his back to the work himself. He knew all too well that his life, and those of his men, all depended on these walls resisting the British guns when they came.

Clearly, Colonel Moultrie, the commander of Fort Sullivan, was also concerned. From the moment that the dawn's light was bright enough to see by, until the last rays of the sun disappeared over Charles Town, the men labored under the merciless early summer sun.

As the supply of fresh timbers coming from the mainland dwindled under the tightening British siege to the north of the city, Corporal Harris and his men were shifted from laying posts and sections, to filling and moving sand bags to back up the flimsy wooden palisade.

Filling one burlap bag after another with wet sand, in a seemingly endless procession of rough cloth and back-breaking shoveling, Justin's thoughts drifted back to Elizabeth and the children, and the farm, where he had thought he knew the meaning of a hard day's work.

He was surprised to find himself longing for the simple pleasure of Terrance's quiet, confident competence. In comparison with some of the men on Sullivan's Island with him, Justin's negro was a paragon of reliability and efficiency. Terrance would not drive a spade full of sand through the bottom of a sack, nor would he leave a shovel on the beach below the high tide line, never to be seen again.

Justin also grew annoyed with the men in his work detail who seemed to want to chatter incessantly, about wenches and drink and favorite places to fish and hunt, and... well, it seemed to Justin as though they never exhausted the possibilities for idle conversation. Terrance asked questions or made comments about the work at hand, but didn't find it necessary to fill every silence with any little thing that popped into his head.

But, most of all, Justin found a new appreciation for the fact that Terrance was never one to shy away from hard work. He didn't complain when the sun beat down, nor was he one to sneak off and take a nap in a shady spot. When the weather took an unpleasant turn, Terrance would keep up with his tasks, even as the rain sloughed off of his back, quietly, competently and without complaint.

Justin knew, too, that this was not just because Terrance

was his property—plenty of slaves had to be beaten, cajoled and threatened every bit as much as the men he was working with now, in order to get a decent day's work out of them. There were one or two men in his detail, though, whom he wouldn't mind being able to send south...

Several days after the British fleet was spotted, Justin was surprised to see the teamster Cooper coming down the beach, wearing the colors of Moultrie's command.

Cooper greeted him, shaking his hand solemnly. "Corporal Harris, I'm pleased to find you."

"Mister—excuse me, Private Cooper. It is an honor to serve with you. I am glad to see you've joined up."

"Speaking with you, Corporal, made me realize that my place was here, not out dodging British patrols in the palmetto stands."

"I am pleased to have played a part, Private Cooper."

"Corporal Harris, I come bearing tidings of your family in Charles Town. Can we go somewhere to talk, undisturbed?" Justin's blood ran cold at this, but he maintained his outward composure.

"Certainly, just let me speak to the detail for a moment." Justin spoke to his most trustworthy man briefly, and then motioned Cooper over to a completed part of the wall.

"Okay, what news have you?"

"Jeremiah Harris, the indigo plantation owner, was killed last week."

Justin felt his face go white at the news. "And his family? What happened?"

"An Irish indentured servant put a knife in him as he slept.

His wife heard the ruckus and got the children out of the plantation house before the servant put it to the torch." Justin's shoulders sagged as he said a prayer of thanks for the safety of Anna and the children, and one for the soul of the man to whom he owed a debt of gratitude, no matter his opposition to his cousin's views.

He remembered the servant, too, and was surprised at the thought that the young woman, who had made no real impression on him, could have committed such a heinous act.

"He was a loyalist to the end, but he was my cousin, and, in his own way, a good man. Was the servant captured?"

"Yes, and hanged that same morning, may God have mercy on her. She's not the only Irish servant to have turned on a Tory master, but most have simply committed acts of sabotage, or have assisted the rebellion in other ways. Few have gone so far as to cold-blooded murder, never mind arson. An act like that does the cause of the Whigs no good."

"No, it surely doesn't. Are the family safe now?"

"I believe so. They are staying in town, with a Whig family—Thomas Harris, I believe?"

"Yes, I know him—not well, but I know him. I... I just hope that Anna and the children are finding some comfort with his family. Those poor children..." Justin's voice cracked, and he turned away from Cooper while he regained his composure.

Turning back to face the other man, he said, "Thank you for bringing me this news, unwelcome though it is. I need to get back to the task at hand, though. Each of us has our private sorrows in this time of trial."

"Indeed, Corporal Harris. Please accept my condolences for your family's loss."

Justin acknowledged Cooper with a nod and a firm handshake, and then walked back up the beach to return to his work detail. As he labored beside his men for the rest of the afternoon, though, he found that his mind was back on the verandah with Jeremiah and his wife. They had come to see him off on his last return home from their plantation, after another pleasant breakfast with the whole family.

Jeremiah had clasped Justin's arm in his hand, and had said to him, "Don't worry overmuch about this rebellion, cousin. The King's men will put things right again in no time, and those of us who remained loyal will be rewarded at the expense of those who turned against the Crown. Mark my words, Justin, this will turn out well in the end."

Justin reflected, sadly, that the King's men had not been able to spare Jeremiah his fate. He wondered what had spurred the servant to act with such violence against the family that had provided her passage to the Colonies and employment upon her arrival. That Irish indentures were unreliable in Tory families was, as Cooper had said, not that unusual—given the bad blood between the English and their Irish subjects, it was to be expected that they would tend to side with the independence-minded colonists.

This, though, as Cooper had said, went beyond the normal antipathy between the two peoples. Knowing his cousin's lack of regard for his slaves and servants, Justin did not doubt that Jeremiah had somehow given the girl additional motivation for her act of savagery. Nonetheless, his cousin had been kind to Justin, and the man's generosity had made a great difference in his life.

Of course, too, with this news, Justin could not help but wonder how things fared with his own wife and children.

Elizabeth's letters were a welcome distraction from the rigors of military life, but he still worried about the British or colonial loyalists learning who had attacked their men in the meadow and taking revenge against them. He fervently prayed for their safety as he shoveled heavy, wet sand into yet another rough burlap bag.

# Chapter 17

Katie sat on the front porch, a mug of coffee steaming in one hand and the phone in the other. She had already left two messages for George Branton but had not said anything to Gram yet. There didn't seem to be any sense in upsetting her grandmother until she had a better idea of how serious the challenge was that Professor Schulmann had raised.

Finally, the phone rang, and the caller ID showed that it was from the University. Katie answered, "Harris residence, Katie Harris speaking."

"Hi, Katie," came George's tired-sounding voice. "I've just tracked down the clip on their Web site, and yes, Schulmann is a Yankee bastard who's given many of us in this field a hard time in the past. Basically, if Saint Jefferson didn't do a thing, it didn't really happen, in his view."

"So, what do you make of his claim that the *Mercury* was not even in publication at that time?"

"Obviously, he's mistaken." Katie released her breath, unaware until then that she'd been holding it.

George continued, "Not only did you hold in your hands a copy from that period, but we have previously seen contemporary records that show that the paper continued to be printed right up through the fall of 1775. While your issue may be the latest one we have extant at this time, I'm fully confident that, with lab analysis,

Schulmann's criticisms will be shown to be baseless."

"Oh, man, I am glad to hear that, George. I was worrying all night. And I am so angry at that snotty so-and-so for insinuating that I forged that newspaper! I am *really* looking forward to proving him wrong, and making him eat his words."

"He's not the type, Katie. Once he's been proven wrong here, he'll move on to harassing somebody else. The media won't care—so long as he's willing to say something outrageous, they'll put his weasel face on the air."

"Oh, he is awful. And his *voice*! He sounds like he's from Brooklyn or something, and just full of resentment over whatever."

George laughed, "Yeah, somebody took away his lunch pail in grade school a few too many times, I think."

Katie sighed, trying not to laugh with the relief she felt. "How do you think that I should discuss this with Gram? She hasn't seen the interview yet."

"Well, I think she can handle it. She knows for certain that you didn't forge the newspaper, so you don't have to worry about that, at least. Just tell her that this happens sometimes, and it's nothing to worry about, in the long run."

"Okay, will do. Thanks a million, George. I feel so much better!"

"No problem, Katie. It's all going to work out just fine."

"Thanks again. Talk to you later."

"Bye, Katie. Keep the faith."

Just then, Gram came in to put her coffee mug into the sink.

"Hi, Gram."

"Hello, Katie. You look worried, dear."

"I spoke to George this morning, and he said it's nothing to worry about, but I'm still angry about something I saw on the news last night."

"Oh? What was that?"

"Some so-called 'expert' said that I must have forged that newspaper. I guess that the guy is a pretty constant thorn in the side of researchers, but he's claiming the newspaper was no longer around by the date of the issue we found."

"It sounds as though he was simply misinformed, Katie. I don't see why you're letting him bother you. After all, you know the truth of the matter, and so do I. And as soon as he gets a chance to look at the paper, he'll be able to see that it's real, which will settle it."

"I don't think he even wants to look at it. He seemed to just want to have the camera on him so he can cast aspersions. Oh, Gram, it wasn't what he said so much as *how* he said it. He made me out to be some kind of liar and cheat, and you know that's just not me!"

Katie's eyes were brimming now with angry tears, and she wiped them away impatiently.

"Oh, my little Katydid, I know, I know," said Gram, as she walked over and embraced Katie, stroking her hair and comforting her. Katy relaxed gradually, her grandmother's touch working its magic for her.

"From what George said, this professor makes a career out of attacking people, and his whole motivation is to get in front of the camera."

"He sounds like a thoroughly unpleasant man," Gram

observed.

The phone rang again, and Katie picked it up—George calling back. She said, "Hi, George, what's up?"

"I've been talking to Bill about it this morning, and he thinks we can probably assemble a preliminary rebuttal in short order, pulling together those references I mentioned to answer Schulmann's primary charge. That will find its way into our formal paper on the document, so it's a good effort to go through anyway—his nonsense just moves up when we get it done. "

"Sounds good," Katie said.

George continued, "The most persuasive evidence, though, will come from testing of the materials themselves. Some of that testing will involve destroying a very small portion of the page on which the Declaration is printed, so we'll need to get your grandmother's written permission before we proceed with that."

"Sure, I don't think she'll have any problem with that."

"Okay. Now, once we've analyzed the paper and the ink, and authenticated them, there should really be no question any longer. Semantic analysis of the content of the newspaper, and, in particular, of the Declaration, will also help, but the physical analysis will nail it down beyond any doubt."

"How long will those take?"

"The semantic analysis could be wrangled over for years, going back and forth between different teams of researchers. The physical analysis should only take a few weeks, though, so by the end of the month, we should have a pretty solid case for the sales value of the document, at least."

"Yes, we need to get this settled before she even decides what to do with the document, I guess."

"Exactly.  In any case, we should have a preliminary statement ready regarding the question of publication dates by tomorrow at the latest, and we may be able to pull that together before the end of the day."

George gave a low chuckle, with a note of menace in it. "I must admit that I would not mind one bit seeing Schulmann take some lumps over this.  He's got Bill and I scrambling, and we shouldn't have needed to."

Katie puttered around the house, working with Gram on repairing the damage to her gardens throughout the morning. The women made sandwiches together for lunch and discussed Schulmann's heritage, grooming and some choice possibilities for an appropriate fate.  Gram had some delightful ideas involving fire ant hills, and Katie's sides hurt from laughing by the time she cleared the table.

# Chapter 18

Justin trudged through the woods behind the bent back of the man in front of him. The summer heat was oppressive with a rucksack on his back and a rifle slung over his shoulder, and his spirit was as weary as his body. His side still ached where a British bullet had grazed him the prior week on Sullivan's Island.

Likewise, his heart ached for the sad letter he had had to send home to Elizabeth, informing her that Prescott, who had already lost so much to the British, had given all in that same battle, and lay with a handful of his fellows who had fallen in the stunning victory over an overwhelming British force.

By rights, he knew, he should be exultant at the fact that the fort still stood, that the soft palmetto trunks had turned out to be ideally suited to absorbing the blows from British cannon. He should be thrilled that a spirited young soldier had given inspiration to all of Charleston by re-mounting the fort's banner, which had fallen to a stray cannonball.

And he knew that he should be proud that the British fleet had lost one of its proudest ships to the bar at Sullivan's Island, never mind that they had been forced to retreat in disarray, both their seaborne and land attacks repulsed by patriot forces that had been outnumbered, outgunned and outmaneuvered by the British at every turn.

Yet, his heart was still heavy at the thought of the acts that he had committed and had seen committed against men who, just a few short years ago, would have been allies and defenders of the Colonies. He was filled with sadness and anger at the King and Parliament that refused to so much as grant the American Colonies' petitions for just the rights of ordinary Englishmen.

The loss, the sheer waste of good men like Prescott, was horrible to contemplate, as was the loss of the men on whom Justin had fired, knocking them down one after another, like tobacco plants after the harvest, off to molder in their premature graves.

The sudden sting of the bullet that had hit him had registered before he even understood that the buzzing bee sound he heard at the same instant had been the bullet in flight toward him. It marked an injury sudden and permanent, while the anguish of watching men die around him and before him had been more gradual and slow to build.

Both now sapped his strength and left him wondering if he had made the right choice. Too, his brief visit with Anna in Charles Town had been deeply sobering. His cousin's wife, who once had graciously received him in her kitchen and at her table, now practically spat in his face upon seeing him with the patriot's trefoil hat on his head.

She seemed to hold him personally responsible for the tragedy which had befallen her family and was no longer the lively, happy woman he had known before. Bitterness and rage at the rebellious Whigs animated her now, and she was all too happy to explain to Justin just how her husband had died and what horrors had followed.

"That mongrel dog of an Irish serving-woman did not just

quietly slip a blade between my husband's ribs in the night, but instead slit his throat like a hog for the slaughter, Justin," she had said, tears streaming anew down her face.

"What's more, the witch splashed his blood over herself in some sort of a gleeful rage, keening and screaming imprecations at Jeremiah as he lay dying. I heard the racket and went to his door and I saw the girl standing there with the blade still wet and red in her hand."

Anna now regarded Justin through reddened eyes narrowed in hatred. "I escaped then with my life and got the children to safety as she took a faggot from the kitchen fireplace and ran through the entire house, setting everything she passed ablaze. The witch never stopped shrieking, Justin, from that moment until they hanged her in front of the smoking ruins. Truly, she was possessed by some sort of demon, but God will have no mercy on her for the acts that she has committed."

Anna stood and pointed commandingly through the door of the room. "Go now, *cousin*. Leave this house of your family and never return. You have besmirched a proud name by joining with these rebels, and I do not believe that any of us ever want to see your face again." He fled, her words echoing cruelly in his ears, feeling more isolated and unsure of himself than he had since he had pulled the trigger on that fateful day in the glade near his home.

Visiting Jeremiah's plantation, he found the great house a blackened and collapsed ruin and the fields already returning to a state of nature, the indigo being overtaken by reeds and grasses. A rough gallows still stood before the house, where the Irish girl had met her own end. There was no sign of the negroes who had once tended the property, and whom Terrance had once counted as his friends and kin.

His one relief was that the militia had been sent home, told to keep itself in a state of readiness, but their immediate duties had been discharged for the moment. So Justin now walked for home with his fellow townsmen, glad at least for the knowledge that he would soon see his wife, children and farm again.

Of course, he and the others would resume their patrol duties around the district with Gauthier, but the British defeat at Sullivan's Island seemed to have ended their designs on the South-Carolina Colony for the moment. Georgia was still threatened, though, and, of course, the New England Colonies were now suffering the brunt of the British military might.

With all of these thoughts heavy in his heart, and the purpling and yellowed bruise that spread out from the welt on his side aching, Justin was hardly in an ideal frame of mind when an officer of the militia rode up alongside the walking column and pulled up by him.

The officer called out, "Corporal Justin Harris?"

"Yes, sir, that is I," replied Justin wearily.

"The colonel has sent for you, Corporal, if you would be so kind as to accompany me?"

"Certainly, sir," Justin answered, wondering what this might portend.

He swung into a jog, ignoring the protests of his injured side and following the officer back to the rear of the column where the command group rode in close formation, their horses walking easily and slowly to keep pace with the walking men ahead of them.

Justin swept off his hat and bowed slightly as he walked alongside the group, addressing the commanding officer. "Colonel

Thompson, sir, Corporal Harris reporting as requested."

"Very good to see you, Corporal. I have had reports of your calm action under fire, even as you were yourself wounded. I wished to recognize your actions, which, if I understand them fully, were instrumental to our success in the recent engagement."

"Sir, I appreciate that deeply, although I think that I only did what any man in the regiment would—and did—do under the circumstances."

"Nevertheless, Corporal, it is you who rose to the occasion, and helped to ensure that the British were turned back, and that rather a large number of them will never see the shores of England again."

Justin's blood ran cold at this bald assessment of the impact of his actions registered. Indeed, the sweetness of the return home that he anticipated for himself within a few more days would never come for the men he had drawn into his sights and had felled.

With a shudder, he answered, "Sir, I take no delight in that knowledge. It was an unfortunate, even tragic, necessity in the situation, but I do not doubt that I killed good men back there, along with the bad, and only chance made them our enemies"

"That, Corporal, is why your actions were so remarkable, as a matter of fact," replied the colonel. He sighed, pausing a long moment. "Harris, I know how difficult it is to fight against our own countrymen. Indeed, I believe that the issue will only become more acute as this war continues—some of our own neighbors in these Colonies will probably take up arms against us, and we may end up facing kin across the battle lines."

The officer sighed. "No, that is why you deserve this commendation, Corporal. You did not fire on those men without thought, merely on the orders of men such as myself. You did so with the knowledge of what your actions meant, and what the results would be. That you did so despite your own injuries gives me the excuse I need to reward you—but I want you to know what I am actually commending you for."

Justin did not know quite what to say, other than to stammer, "Thank you, sir," and accept the sealed parchment the colonel held out to him.

"I wish that I could do something more meaningful, Corporal Harris, but this is what is within my power. When you have reached home, enjoy your hearth and kin as much as you can, for one never knows when your country may need you again. That is all, Corporal; you may return to your position."

Jogging back past the column of men to the rank where he had been walking before, Justin found that the colonel's words had, in fact, lightened his heart, if only a little. It was good to know that he was not alone in the worries that had occupied his mind as his feet had mechanically moved one step after the next.

Swinging his rucksack off his back as he continued to walk along, Justin slipped the commendation into it, still unopened, to preserve it for his wife and children to see when he arrived home. The woods seemed somehow brighter now, and his pains were no longer so wearing. He began to think of the moment of seeing his Elizabeth, and their children, and that thought lifted his heart even further.

He stopped noticing the sweat trickling down his neck, and started listening to the birdsong in the woods around him, and the occasional high screech of a cicada. The miles ahead seemed less difficult than those behind, and, for the first time in a week, Justin

Harris smiled a bit as he walked.

A few days later, walking over the rise to where he could first see the house again, after an absence of several months, Justin felt the relief and comfort of seeing his well-ordered fields, nearly ready for the harvest, and his house, trim and tidy, with a serene curl of smoke rising from the chimney.

As he drew closer, Justin again felt a sense of disquiet, but he could not identify what might be causing it. He lengthened and quickened his stride, entering the house, where Timothy and his sister were playing quietly just inside the door.

He set his rucksack beside the doorway, and they jumped up and greeted him enthusiastically, as was usual upon his return from briefer trips to Charles Town, but as his eyes adjusted to the low light in the room, Justin saw that Elizabeth was sitting listlessly in her chair, her hair in disarray, her red and puffy eyes only rising briefly to note his arrival.

His heart gripped with icy fear, he disentangled his legs from the children, rushed to her and knelt, taking her hands in his. "What is it, Elizabeth? Whatever is the matter?"

Her voice broke as she replied, "The baby, Justin. Patrick was taken with fever a fortnight ago, and..." she began to sob quietly, her shoulders quaking under Justin's hands as he embraced her. "...he's gone," she wailed. His own tears began to flow as he held her close.

Weeping into his shoulder, she regained her voice, "Then I got your letter and I was terrified that you would not return, and that I would be left here alone, and—" She clutched him tightly, sobbing aloud now. The children watched, solemn and silent, the sight of the two pillars of their lives in such disarray completely outside of their experience.

Justin stroked Elizabeth's hair and said simply, "I am here. I am here." His tears ran in sheets down his cheeks from under closed eyelids, and he found himself wondering just what the point of it all was, if a child could be snatched away without warning, if a good man could lose everything, and then lose his life, if men who yesterday were brothers could today become sworn enemies... surely their Maker had some intent, some reason, some sense... but Justin could not discern it, not just now.

After what seemed to him an eternity, Justin fought to compose his face, wiping tears away with his sleeve. His voice still unsteady, he asked, "Where—where is he?"

Elizabeth answered in a lifeless tone, "Terrance dug the grave, under the big oak behind the house... the pastor came out and said the service for us... everything is done that needed to be done... the rest of us were never even taken with a fever... oh, Justin, thank God that you are returned safe!"

"I need to go see him, Elizabeth. I will be back in a little while." Justin rose and walked numbly through the doorway. He turned, barely conscious of his body as he seemed to float around the house to where the sun dappled the ground under the spreading limbs of the oak. Amongst a bed of brilliant yellow flowers at its base, a tiny mound of disturbed soil marked with a simple cross drew him inexorably forward, until he stood beside his son's grave.

What purpose, he asked God in his heart, was served by tearing away a man's son? What grand scheme, even beyond mortal vision, could be fulfilled by such a senseless event? How did God want him to learn from this, to glorify His name, out of all of the horror he had seen and perpetrated of late?

Justin was not even aware that he was on his knees, shouting to the sky, until Terrance's arm was around his shoulders, a steady, silent presence while Justin's entire being seemed to be sliding into an abyss of sorrow and lament. His throat was raw from screaming, and his tears had long since run dry when he finally started to be aware of his surroundings again.

As he slowly came back to his senses, he looked at the negro's face, where he saw his own pain reflected in Terrance's features. The slave spoke now, his deep voice as sad as Justin had ever heard any man's sound. "I am sorry, Mister Harris. I did everything Missus Harris asked me to, and everything I could think to do, but the baby just... it was as if God had spoken to him, Mister Harris, and told him it was time to come home... and he just did."

He shook his head slowly, as if in disbelief, repeating, "I am sorry." He stood slowly and walked back to his work in the field, leaving Justin alone with his grief once again. Justin leaned heavily against the gnarled bark on the trunk of the old tree, feeling its solid presence under his hand. Leaning against the tree, he pushed himself upright again in slow stages.

After saying a prayer over his son's grave, Justin turned his back on the mounded earth where the baby now rested, and returned to his wife and the two older children inside the house.

He spent the next few days moving woodenly through his routines. He emptied out his rucksack, placing the now-meaningless commendation into Elizabeth's blanket chest, in a satchel with the broadside that had so enraged Jeremiah. He labored in the fields, alongside Terrance once again, taking quiet pleasure in the other man's competence and hard work.

Telling Elizabeth about Jeremiah's fate, and his ejection

from the security of his extended family's care and concern had been a difficult duty, although she seemed to be recovering from Patrick's death now that she had Justin back home safe and mostly sound. Terrance had not reacted outwardly when Justin mentioned to him the fate of his former master, but had shown concern when he learned that the slaves from the plantation were no longer there, but Justin knew nothing about their whereabouts to share with the negro.

Elizabeth had clucked over his wound, and had insisted upon preparing a poultice to apply to it, sending Terrance out into the woods to gather birch bark and a collection of herbs. In truth, Justin found, it did help with the fading ache of the bruising across his side, and within a day or two, he was feeling almost completely recovered from the physical damage he had endured.

A week after the regiment had returned home, Harold Gauthier came around to the farm. "I heard in town, Justin. I am sincerely sorry for your loss. God is cradling your son in His arms, waiting for you to come and claim him in your own turn."

Justin nodded, still struggling with the fact of Patrick's death. "Thank you for reminding me of that, Harold." He squared his shoulders and took a deep breath. "What is the status of the Committee of Safety? Do we still patrol the district?"

"We do, Justin, but we can manage without you for a while, if you need."

"No, Harold, I've seen men whose lives lay in ruins about them out on the lines, doing their duties. I cannot do any less. When am I needed?"

Harold drew in a long breath and then blew it out, shaking his head. "You can take the eastern loop at dawn tomorrow, Justin.

Thank you."

Once again on the mare, riding the familiar circuit, Justin found himself in the same clearing where he had fired his own first shot of the Revolution. His curiosity got the better of him, and he went to examine the place where the Redcoat had fallen. He located the spot where their campfire must have been, and his gaze fell upon a rude cross of two branches fastened together, standing at the head of a long, low mound in the dirt.

He felt a chill come over him as he realized that this was where the man he had killed now lay. The enormity of what had passed in just a few short months rushed over him, and a vision of a long row of graves and crosses swam before his eyes, each marking the spot where the remains of a human life he had snuffed out lay. At the very end of the row was the tiny mound over his son, and Justin knew that he was responsible for this grave, too.

He did not remember his flight back to the village this time, either, but he did find his way into the tavern, where he sat heavily in the same seat where Harold Gauthier had spoken to him about being a soldier or being a farmer, where Justin had taken the second step on the road to raising a cemetery's worth of graves, where the innkeeper offered forgiveness in the form of cup after cup of rough corn whiskey, after the rum had run out.

Eventually, Justin stood, belched and very deliberately and methodically made his way back to the mare, tucking two jugs of liquor into his saddlebag before mounting up and letting her take him home. Fortunately, the mare knew the roads and paths as well as he, and needed no guidance from her master, who snored on her neck until Terrance reached up and helped him down from the saddle.

Justin later had little memory of the following weeks. Although the critical season of the tobacco harvest was upon them, Justin did nothing at all in the fields, lying in a stupor through most of the day, rousing himself only to return to the tavern and exchange empty jugs for full. Elizabeth attended to him and cared for the children in quiet desperation, praying every night that whatever demons haunted her husband would relinquish their hold on him.

And then, one day, Justin returned from the village without the jugs. Harold Gauthier had been waiting for him at the tavern, and had invited him to sit for a drink.

"Tell me what you are doing, Justin," the older man had said, gravely.

"I'm staying busy," Justin slurred in response.

"I haven't seen you at the Committee meetings, nor have you been on your patrol, but for that first day."

"There's no need," replied Justin. "They're dead. All dead. I killed them all, one after another." He began to weep. "I killed them, Harold! *Their* wives won't greet them with relieved smiles and welcoming arms. *Their* children won't cling to their pants and cry out in joy to see Papa again. *Their* mothers won't hold their sons close and thank Providence for sparing them. No, I saw to that, one, two, three! Down they fall! Four, five, six! Can't even count them, so many! I killed all of them, the British soldiers, the cousin who loved me and gave me everything I needed, the son who wanted only to climb into my lap and be held—" Justin's voice broke and he collapsed onto the table, sobbing uncontrollably.

Gauthier regarded his friend sadly and with patience, finally speaking quietly to him. "Justin, you did what had to be done, at every turn. The men you shot—every one of them—would have killed you, had they had the chance. That was what they were sent here to do, to crush the rebellion you were a part of. If you had not killed them, Elizabeth would have gotten a letter and a memorial instead of her husband when we came back from Charles Town."

"As for your cousin, he died at the hands of a serving girl who had had enough of being diddled by the master."

Justin's head shot up and he regarded Gauthier with fury. "How dare you say that about Jeremiah Harris, you—you—"

"I say it because that is what the jury heard from her own lips after they sentenced her to hang by the neck until dead. She had nothing to gain by lying at that point, and from what other people have told me about your cousin, he wasn't one to spend much thought on the what those who served him wanted or deserved from him. He may have treated you with kindness, but he never wasted any of that on his slaves or indentures."

Justin's shoulders slumped as he acknowledged the truth of Gauthier's words. "As for your son, Justin, nothing would have been any different if you had been home working in your fields. He would have taken ill, you and Elizabeth would have done everything you could think of to save him, and he would be buried under the oak, all just the same. When the Lord is ready to take a soul into His grace, nothing we do here can change His mind. Patrick's time came, and that was all there was to it."

"You cannot change any of these things, either. What is past is done, and cannot be undone. All that you can change is what you do with *right now*. And, frankly, what you're doing is going to wind up killing Elizabeth. She feared she had lost you once, Justin, but you came back. Now, she is losing you again, right before her eyes, and she has got to know that you will not come back this time, if you continue down this path."

Justin looked up again and regarded the other man blearily. "I can't ask Elizabeth to bear any more than she already has, Harold. She is a good woman, better than I deserve. You are right, I am killing her. I'm killing her, too, Harold!" His head fell onto his arms again as he wept anew.

After several minutes he finally raised his eyes to look at Gauthier. "Harold, what can I do? How can I be worthy of her again? What must I do?"

"Justin, you must get back on your horse and go home and sleep until you are sober. Then you must get up, get back to work and accept the grace of God that will fill you. You are worthy, both of Elizabeth and of that grace, and you will regain both the instant you walk out of this tavern."

Justin absorbed this, and then silently rose and shuffled out of through the door to his waiting mare. Gauthier sighed deeply and stood to follow him into the muggy afternoon, waving to the innkeeper, who waved back with a slightly rueful expression on his face.

Arriving home, Justin handed the reins of his mare to Terrance, as had been his habit of late, and went into the house, where he made for the bed without saying anything. When he woke, the he felt the need to step outside, and he rose quietly, not disturbing any of his family as he did so.

After he finished his business, he stood for a while, looking into the heavens. The oppressive heat of the day had given way to a velvety warmth, and the skies were clear, the stars cheerfully twinkling down at him.

Without being conscious of it, he found that his steps led

him to the old oak tree, where grass was already sprouting over the mounded earth where the baby lay. Justin stood over the grave, deep in thought, for what seemed an eternity. By the time he returned to his bed, the eastern horizon was already purple with the first glimmer of dawn.

He awoke again in mid-morning and walked slowly up into the tobacco fields, his head pounding. He was shocked to see that the harvest was done, and, looking wonderingly to the drying shed, he found the sticks of tobacco leaves all hung neatly, curing for market. Terrance was nowhere in sight, off doing some errand, seeing to the running of the farm, just as he had when Justin had been gone altogether.

Justin found himself wracked with guilt for his conduct over the past weeks. He returned to the house, where he found Elizabeth stripping corn from the ears, her strong arms making quick work of the hard job. The children were amusing themselves by chasing down stray kernels, laughing and shrieking as they bounced and ricocheted around the room. Justin's face registered pain with every high-pitched squeal, but he said nothing to them.

He sat across the table from Elizabeth and just watched her for a while, saying nothing. He noticed, with sadness, that her brow now bore furrows from worry, and her eyes had a new, pinched cast about them. Her mouth, once perpetually laughing, was now set in a grim line of concentration as she labored over the corn.

Finally, she spoke, not looking away from what she was doing. "Are you feeling better, Justin?" He thought he heard an edge to her voice, but he could not blame her if she were angry.

"I am, Elizabeth," he said simply. She continued to work,

not looking at him, and his eyes brimmed with unshed tears. "I don't know where I've been since I came home. I have been... weak." The children fell quiet as they heard his voice, and Elizabeth motioned them outside with a tilt of her head.

Now she faced him, looking into his eyes steadily, her hands still busy with the work. "I have been waiting here for you, Justin. You might have come back from battle, but you brought it home within you. I understand that. You have seen things that I cannot even imagine. I understand that. I thank God daily that I have been able to manage this house without you, and that your cousin, God rest his soul, made it possible for me to manage the farm in your absence."

She began to cry quietly now, too. "I have prayed that you would be delivered of the ghosts which have haunted you since you returned from Charles Town. My heart is gladdened to see you sitting before me without reeking of whiskey. I hope that you are back to stay."

"I am, Elizabeth," Justin quietly replied. He reached out and took one of her hands in his, just holding it for a long, long time, as they both sat with their eyes closed, each feeling the strength of the other's presence. Eventually, Justin released her hand.

"I'm going to get to work, Elizabeth. There's a lot that needs doing, I'm sure." He rose and went outside to find Terrance and see what was to be done.

He found the negro in the garden plot, harvesting the last of the corn. Justin sat in the relative cool of the shade of the house with a sack that Terrance had filled, and started husking the corn, putting the husks into one basket and then stripping away the silk and putting the cleaned ears of corn into another. After several minutes' work, he spoke to Terrance.

"I owe you a debt of gratitude, Terrance. I saw the work you did on the tobacco harvest, and I could not have done any better myself."

"I am glad that I did it all right, Mister Harris," Terrance replied.

"I have no excuse, Terrance, for what I've done in the past few weeks, and I know that it has fallen most heavily on you to make up for my shortcomings."

"Mister Harris... I know that you have gone through the very gates of hell, and came back bearing some of that hellfire in your soul." Terrance stopped working and came over to sit beside Justin. He looked intently into the white man's eyes, his own filled with pain as he continued. "I know what it takes out of a man to go to such a place. My eldest son, he was sold with his mother down to Savannah, a year or two before you bought me. I never saw either of them again, and I never will, either."

Terrance took a deep breath. "My other boy was the child I saw bit by a snake, Mister Harris. My father, like I said, he did everything he knew how to do, but the boy didn't make it. Now, you come back from Charles Town and tell me that the whole plantation is gone, and you have no idea what might have happened to my family and my friends."

"Mister Harris, I know, and I don't mind what I've had to do while you fought your demons. You and I, we have each gone through hard times, and I know how you feel. I know that you are a good master, and a good man, and that you will do the right thing when the time comes. You always have, and I trust that you always will."

Justin sat, stunned at the revelations from his slave. In this man's breast beat a heart at least as scored by sadness as his own. He felt a moment's anger at himself as he realized that Terrance had borne up better under the burdens that fate had placed on him than he had.

Justin was about to speak when he heard the approaching hoofbeats and jangling tack of a man on horseback. As he drew closer, Justin recognized Reverend Le Tourneau from the Huguenot congregation in town. The man dismounted and Justin rose from his stool to go and greet him.

"Good morning, Reverend," Justin said.

"Good day to you, Justin. I expect that your return home has felt like a bit of a mixed blessing, and I wish that I had been here to greet you upon your return. In any event, I thought that I should come on by and sit with you and your family for a bit."

"I thank you for that, Reverend. Yes, I have been... feeling poorly for a while, but I am doing considerably better now."

Justin motioned to Le Tourneau to follow him to the benches in front of the house, leaving Terrance to work alone again for the moment.

"Still, I know that there are many men who, having experienced what you've gone through, would simply fall apart completely, would be overwhelmed by the demons you have wrestled with. Clearly, you have overcome them, and you are to be commended for that."

"I... I have been weak, Reverend."

"You have been human, Justin, and God forgives us for that, since He made us that way."

"But can He forgive me for the things I have done,

Reverend? Is not warfare against our brothers a sin? Isn't one of God's Commandments, 'Thou shalt not kill?' Does he excuse us just because we have been set upon a path on which we see no other choice?"

"Ah, Justin, we do live in difficult days for that Commandment. We are blessed, however, by the boundless forgiveness of Jesus for our sins—from the least to the worst of them. God knows your heart, He knows your soul, and will not hold against you the sins that you have asked His forgiveness for."

"I cannot easily comprehend forgiveness, Reverend, for putting those who were not so long ago my countrymen into early graves."

"Yes, Justin, precisely. God's forgiveness is beyond our comprehension. But you may rely upon it nonetheless. I assure you—you *are* forgiven, as surely as you were born."

Justin drew a deep breath and released it, closing his eyes as he considered this idea. He knew that he had heard the same thing all his life, but it had always been an abstract concept before now. To be told that he was granted forgiveness for the horrors he had watched himself commit...

As if the Reverend could hear his thoughts, he said, "I know that the most difficult part of God's forgiveness can be simply accepting it, Justin. But I know, too, from experience, that as soon as you ask it... you will know that it is granted. You don't need to ask me for it—just ask Him, in your heart, and you will learn immediately that He is listening and ready for your prayer. That is all you need do."

Justin nodded. "I shall, Reverend. I will confess that I feel unworthy of anyone's forgiveness, but if, as you say, God finds me worthy, I will... ask Him myself."

"It is all that you need do, Justin. I will pray that you will feel the touch of the Holy Spirit in that moment—that you will feel your guilt fall away just as you feel the relief when you shed a coat heavy with rain when you come inside. Christ is waiting, Justin, and He is patient. You need only call on Him through prayer."

"Thank you, Reverend. I do appreciate it." Justin took another bracing, deep breath and blew it out. "I feel better already, in truth." He thought for a moment longer, then asked, "Tell me this, though: is it possible that God took my youngest son in retribution for my sin of taking away other fathers' sons?"

"It may seem so to you, but God is forgiving, not vengeful. If you have sinned against him, he will not punish your son. Calling Patrick home was doubtless a part of His plan that we cannot completely understand, but I assure you that it was not a punishment for you for your sins, either."

"I wish that I could understand that, Reverend. And I wish that I had never sinned against God's Commandment, so that I could be certain in my heart that my son's loss was truly not related."

"You will meet your son again, Justin, and when you do, you will understand what God's plan for him was. Until then, you can only have faith that what Jesus told us was that we are forgiven our sins, and God does not loose his wrath upon us for them. When you come to feel His forgiveness, you will understand this, as well, I am certain."

Justin nodded, swallowing hard, his eyes wet. "I—I just can't bear the thought that I should have been here, that I should have stayed with my family, that I should never have taken up arms, that—"

"Justin," Le Tourneau interrupted him. "You have acted according to God's plan. He has long ago decided down to the smallest little bird what each of our fates should be, and we are powerless before His will. He would not have led you down a path from which there was no redemption, nor would He have set you on a road to such punishment."

"I... will need to think about that, Reverend, and pray for understanding."

"And I will also pray for your understanding, or at least acceptance of the wisdom of God's plan for you."

"Thank you once again, Reverend."

"You are welcome, Justin. Shall we go inside and speak with your wife?"

The two men went in, and Justin returned to work on the corn shucking. Elizabeth and Reverend Le Tourneau talked for a long time, and when Le Tourneau emerged from the house and bade Justin farewell, the oppressive heat of the noonday sun seemed easier for all on the farm to bear, and the air itself seemed to be lighter on Justin's shoulders.

# Chapter 19

"Hi, Gram," Katie called as she came back into the house.

"Katie, come here, child," Gram called from the kitchen.

"What is it, Gram?" Katie asked as she rounded the corner to see Gram seated at the kitchen table, a cold cup of coffee between her hands.

"Your father called, dear. He's been... hurt." Katie's blood ran cold.

"What? How badly? Is he coming home? What happened?"

"Slow down, Katydid, slow down. Here, sit."

Katie took a seat and then drew a deep breath, trying to calm herself.

"It was some kind of bombing, he said, and he's not badly hurt. He was in a caravan heading to some town—I can't remember the name of it, of course—and the thing went off next to his truck, which flipped right over onto its side."

Gram smiled wryly. "You know your father—he was the only one in the vehicle wearing a safety belt, so he fared better than the driver, who was crushed under the thing. Died instantly, your father said. At least he didn't suffer."

"But what happened to Pop? How badly was he hurt?"

"He said that he probably dislocated his shoulder, and he can't hear out of his right ear at the moment. Katie, he's coming home—the medics on the scene thought that he might have suffered a blast concussion."

Katie's mind raced over all of the different things that she'd read about blast injuries, trying to keep control over a rising swell of panic in her gut. "What does that mean?"

"I'm not sure, and your father couldn't really tell me, either. He did say that he couldn't really remember much about the explosion itself, and he said that seemed to worry the medics. In any case, the firm is sending him home immediately for a full assessment. They've got an agreement with the Army hospital in DC—Walter Reed—and he'll be going there first. Your mother will meet him there, and she should be able to tell us more."

"When will he be back?"

"Tomorrow night, late."

"Good, then I have time to get there, too."

"No, Katie. He told me that he wants you to stay here for the time being."

"Why?"

"He just said that he's in no immediate danger, but he is a mess, and he wants to get patched up a bit before you see him."

Gram shook her head. "He always did want to just be left alone when he hurt himself as a boy, too. Stubborn man. Gets it from your Grandpa. Katie, I'm worried, too, but I know your father. If he thought that there was a chance that you needed to—to come say goodbye, I know that he could want you there. So it's actually good news that he wants you to stay put."

"I guess so," said Katie reluctantly. She sighed deeply,

spreading her hands out on the table before her.

"But Gram, if he's going to be just fine, why are they rushing him all the way back here?"

"I hope that it's just as a precautionary measure, Katie. Of course, I only spoke to your father, so I don't know what the medics there are basing their decisions on. Once he's here, hopefully we can talk to his doctors and they'll tell us that it was an overreaction, and we've just got time to visit with him before he goes back there."

Katie drew a deep sigh, and then nodded agreement. "Okay. So now, we just wait?"

"Now, we wait," Gram agreed, quietly taking Katie's hands. "And pray."

"I'm guessing that we can't call Pop because he's en route, but can I call Mum, or is she already on a plane?"

"She didn't say what her flights would be, so I don't know. Go ahead and try her, if it will make you feel better."

Katie stood and grabbed the phone, dialing quickly. After a moment, she commented to Gram, "Voicemail," and then left a brief message for her mother. She returned to sit with her grandmother, taking her hands again.

"I'm sure you're right, Gram, and everything will be okay. I just wish that I had something more solid to go on, you know?"

"I do, too, Katie. I do, too."

# Chapter 20

As Justin returned to the normal routine of preparing the barrels and packing away the tobacco to bring it to the government house—now in Patriot hands rather than the Crown's—he was struck over and over again at how much Terrance had accomplished, both when Justin was away at the siege of Charles Town, and after his ignominious return.

There was nearly as much tobacco this harvest has there had been the prior year, when both Justin and Terrance had been working the fields. It was all in top-quality condition, as well, so it would fetch a good price, even under strained market conditions.

The rest of the farm was similarly in impressively good repair. To be sure, Elizabeth and even Timothy had each been able to help out to some extent, but Terrance had carried the bulk of the load single-handedly.

Sitting at the supper table a week or so after Reverend Le Tourneau's visit, Justin broached the subject with his wife. "Elizabeth, I cannot help but think that it is an injustice that I sit at a comfortable table with you, eating the wonderful repast you have prepared for our family, while one who made it all possible in my absence... and weakness, sits alone to whatever rude meal he can make of what we give him to subsist upon."

Elizabeth frowned slightly and paused, before replying, "If it is injustice, if his role in this world is misplaced, how could one go about righting that wrong?"

Justin hesitated, then plunged on, "You remember what Samuel Collins did, after his negro Louis pulled the children out of the burning house?"

Elizabeth looked sharply at her husband. "Do you mean to free Terrance, Justin?"

"I am thinking about it, Elizabeth. He has already repaid our investment in him, just in the additional tobacco that he has enabled me to produce. Furthermore, he saved Katherine's life, and would have saved Patrick's, if it had been possible to do so."

Justin looked at the floor, his face starting to burn with shame. "Too, I cannot help but observe that he is a better man than I in many respects. He has endured things that you and I can scarce comprehend, and yet I have never heard him raise one word of complaint. How can I, who have been weak and flawed, persist in the idea that he, who has been strong and constant, should be my *property*, no different from a good steer or a fine rifle?"

Elizabeth put her hand on Justin's arm, comforting him. "My dear, you have been but human, and you have redeemed yourself already in my eyes. I think no less of you for having struggled with your demons—and cast them off!—nor does anybody else."

Her brow furrowed as she was lost in thought for a moment. "What would he do if you released him, Justin? Would we keep him on here?"

"If that were his will, yes, I could gladly keep him on—and pay him a fair wage for his labor. However, I suspect that he might like to see about his family in Charles Town. The letter I have sent to my family there, inquiring on his behalf, has not merited so much as the courtesy of a reply yet. After all," Justin smiled wryly, "I am a damned Whig, and he is but a negro, in their eyes."

"I know, Justin. No, your family is unlikely to be of any particular assistance in that question. I must confess, however, that I fail to see how Terrance could be much more successful on his own."

"He can speak to the slaves on the neighboring plantations—I would gladly give him a letter of introduction for the purpose of securing permission to do so—and learn what they might know."

"That is a worthy thought, Justin." Elizabeth sighed. "I just worry that he would hardly know what to do as a freeman."

"I suspect that he might know better than I, even, what to do with his liberty. Terrance is probably a better man even than I credit him with."

Elizabeth nodded thoughtfully. "Well, if you think that this is the right thing to do, I suppose that you should go into town and get the papers drawn up in the morning." She looked sternly at him, her expression softened with a small twinkle in her eye. "Just don't meet anyone in the tavern, all right?"

He lowered his head gravely. "No, Elizabeth, I misdoubt that I will ever again find my solace in that place."

"I know that, my beloved. Go and bring Terrance in to sit with us, so that we may tell him of your decision... and that he may eat with us, if he likes."

# Chapter 21

"Hello?" Katie tried to keep the fright—no, panic—out of her voice as she answered the phone.

"Hi, Katie," came George's incongruously cheerful voice, "Is something the matter?"

"Yes, George, I'm sorry—my Pop's been hurt overseas, and they're bringing him home now." Once again, Katie could feel her eyes well up as the words underscored the reality of the situation.

"Oh, God, I'm so sorry to hear that, Katie! I hope that everything turns out all right. I'll just call back another time, okay?"

Katie gathered herself for a moment, and then said, "No, George, that's okay." She took a deep breath. "It would be nice to think about something else for a minute."

"If you're sure, Katie …"

"Yes, I'm sure. What were you calling about?"

"I just wanted to keep you posted on our progress in examining the document. We've taken the samples and sent the off to the lab for analysis. Everyone who's looked at the information we've got so far has said that it's all completely consistent with an authentic item. We'll still have to wait for the lab analysis, but I don't think that you have anything to worry about from that Schulmann wart."

Katie took a deep breath, nodding into the telephone. "I

am glad to hear that much good news, at least," she said.

"And I am glad to share it, Katie. I'll let you go now—I am sure that you have bigger things to attend to than this right now."

"Thanks for the update, George."

Almost as soon as they said goodbye and she hung up the phone, it rang again.

"Hello?"

"Hi, Katie," her mother said. "Are you doing all right?"

"Yeah, Mum, I'm okay, and Gram's doing all right at the moment, too. What do you know?"

"I've just landed in Baltimore, and I'll be taking a taxi over to Walter Reed whenever I get off of the phone. I had a voice mail from the firm's medical office while I was in the air, and they were able to give some more details about your father's injuries."

"Go ahead," said Katie, fear clutching at her heart again.

"He probably has a dislocated shoulder, plus some pretty bad bruising and a lot of glass blown into the side of his head from the window. The thing that they're really worried about, though, is that he had some of the initial symptoms, at least, of what they call a traumatic brain injury."

"So what does that mean?"

"Well, it's not terribly well-understood—it's sort of a new type of injury, since it used to be that people that close to any kind of explosion like that would be just—" her voice broke into a sob, and Katie wished with all of her being that she could be there with her mother.

After a moment, her Mum continued, "Most people hit with an explosion like this just wouldn't make it. With better armor and so forth, though, a lot of folks have been surviving it, so they're learning how to treat people who've suffered this sort of injury, and what to expect. They didn't really know much more than that yet—they'll be doing all kinds of assessments and tests and monitoring at Walter Reed—the people there are the best in the world at treating this thing, if it turns out that that's what he's got."

"Okay," Katie said, digesting this. "I guess I can do some research on the net, and see what I can find there."

"Sure," her Mum said, "but don't get panicked about anything you see there—as I said, they told me that this is a rapidly-evolving field, so a lot of what you're going to find out there is just going to be out of date."

"Right, okay," said Katie.

"All right, you going to be good, then, for the time being?"

"Yeah, I think so, Mum." She took a deep, shuddering breath. "Tell Pop I said hello when you see him, will you?"

"Sure thing, Katie, of course. Can I talk to your grandmother now?"

"Sure, just a second." Katie brought the phone in to the living room, where Gram sat, not really reading the paper.

"Mum," Katie said, smiling tensely at Gram and handing her the phone.

"Hello, Kim. What have you heard?"

Katie slipped back into the kitchen to get herself some iced tea while Gram and her Mum spoke. When she came back, Gram was sitting with the phone in her lap, done with the conversation.

"It sounds bad, Gram, but at least he's getting the best care he can, right?"

Gram sighed heavily. "Yes, I suppose that we just have to

trust that they'll do everything that they can for him." She looked up at Katie. "I guess we should have something to eat, don't you think?"

"Yes, I suppose so. Just some soup, maybe, and crackers?"

"Yes, that sounds nice. I'll set the table." Gram stood up painfully from the chair, her eyes pinched shut for a moment until the stiffness eased.

As Katie busied herself heating up a can of tomato soup, Gram moved around the kitchen slowly, and Katie was aware again of just how the years had worn on her grandmother. Although, she reflected, as she ladled the soup into bowls, grated a bit of cheese over it and set crackers on the side of each plate, perhaps it was less the years, and more the accumulated setbacks and difficulties of a long and otherwise happy life.

# *Chapter*  – –

Once again, Justin and Terrance bent their backs together to prepare the sprouting field for a year's tobacco crop. After four years of the same process, the last two as partners rather than as master and slave, they had developed a comfortable routine. Working the sod with their hoes, they broke up clods of dirt, matted with roots from last year's crop and the grass that had overtaken the small field after the sprouts were transplanted.

Neither found it necessary to say anything as they worked. Both focused on breaking the topsoil into even, soft dirt, so that the miniscule tobacco seed could find purchase in it. The warmth of the springtime sun, soaking into the freshly turned earth produced the most wonderful aroma Justin could imagine—the smell of rich, warm loam, ready to receive seed and bring forth new life.

By midday, the work was pretty well finished, and Terrance walked down to the tobacco shed to retrieve the hoarded seed from last fall's crop. Just a few tobacco plants out of the field had been allowed to go to seed, but they had provided all that was needed for this new season.

Justin accepted the sack from Terrance, who now went over to the stream and filled the watering can, returning to wait beside Justin. Justin opened the sack, dipping his hand into the fine, soft seeds and leaning down over the soil to distribute them evenly over the surface. After he had dusted a section of earth with the seeds, he used the flat of his hand to lightly cover them, and Terrance leaned over to gently wet the earth where the seeds now rested.

At the end of the day, both mens' backs ached, but the tobacco planting was done, and they were grateful to sit and take their supper.

As he cleaned his plate with a biscuit, Terrance spoke. "Thank you, Missus Harris. That meal was worth working all day for."

"Thank you, Terrance," said Elizabeth, nodding at the praise. "So," she continued, turning to Justin, "Are you done with the tobacco planting?"

"Yes, we are. We should be able to get the garden field prepared by the end of the week," he answered, anticipating her question. "After that, it will be about time to get the sheep sheared."

Terrance smiled broadly. "I'm going to out-shear you this year, Mister Harris."

"We'll just see about that," laughed Justin. "In any case, it looks like the wool will command good prices again this year. The Continentals in New England have had another hard winter of it, and they're clamoring for good cloth. I only hope that the Royal Navy doesn't intercept another ship at Charles Town harbor."

"How odd it is, that they have scarcely harassed us here in South Carolina, while they batter Georgia and New England," Elizabeth commented.

Justin replied with a brief snort, "You weren't there at Sullivan's Island. They may be right idiots in many regards, but the Redcoats do have memories. They won't soon forget what we did to them there... nor shall I," he finished, the familiar old harrowed look coming into his eyes.

He shook his head to dispel the gathering ghosts, and continued, "I do hope that they will leave us in peace, though as badly as things go in New England, I fear that we will soon all suffer again under the yoke of an angry tyrant."

Elizabeth asked, concern in her voice, "Is it truly as bad as that, Justin?"

He nodded grimly. "The Redcoats and the British Navy have taken Savannah, as I'm sure I've already mentioned. I spoke last week with Tobias Cooper, who had fled when they entered the city, and I dare not tell you of the horrors inflicted upon the populace of that fair town by the conquering forces."

He shook his head sadly. "I dread what they might do to Charles Town, should they take that city which so effectively resisted them once before."

His tone turned angry now. "To think that these Redcoats style themselves as civilized, and jeer at our militias and merchantmen, that they regard themselves as our betters—ha!"

Elizabeth took Justin's hand and stroked it gently, calming him. "Justin, they have convinced themselves that we here in the Colonies are certainly their inferiors, and that gives them license to treat us with inhumanity, in their minds."

She thought for a moment, following the thread of the idea she had in her mind, and then said, "I believe that they have lost this war by doing that, Justin. If their commanders had impressed on them that we colonists are still their countrymen, that we are to be brought to heel, but as gently as possible, they would not have sacked Savannah in the manner that I'm afraid you are declining to describe."

Justin immediately saw what she was saying, and replied, "I think you're right, Elizabeth. They've misunderstood us from the beginning, whether out of malice or simple willful ignorance. Instead of treating us as citizens, they have treated us as subjects, and that makes all the difference, does it not?"

Terrance, who was following the exchange quietly up to this point, chimed in now. "Even the worst slave master knows that those who are beaten harshly will do less work than those who are less heavily disciplined. The British King George does not understand this simple fact, perhaps because there are no slaves in England?"

"Or, perhaps just because he believes that there are no British citizens, only subjects of the Crown. Never mind that that question was settled over five hundred years ago. Small matter, that, to a tyrant who would oppress a distant portion of his nation without due consideration of the effects upon the whole!"

Justin was clearly getting worked up again, and Elizabeth took both of his hands into her own, looking into his eyes and saying in soothing tones, "But if we're right, then the sacrifices borne by the people of Savannah and New England will be the thing that ensures our eventual independence. Having seen what treatment we may expect at the hands of the Crown, what colonist would willingly submit to that again? We will prevail, Justin, though we may still suffer under the power of arms and men for a while longer."

Justin's shoulders slumped. "I hope that you are right, Elizabeth, but I hope, too, that we will not see such evils visited upon South-Carolina. I have not the heart for another fight, but fight I will, if they return to our shores."

He sighed. "For tonight, though, I am weary, and I would join the children in sleep."

He rose from the table. "Good night, Terrance. Sleep well—we have much to do in the morning."

The negro stood and replied, "Good night, Mister Harris, Missus Harris," and then made his way out to his cabin. Elizabeth sat for a short while longer, looking into the embers in the fireplace, then rose from the table and joined her husband where he lay with

# Chapter 23

the children already draping arms and legs over his sleeping form.

Sunlight slanted through a gap in the curtains, creeping across the pillow until it struck Katie directly on her closed eyelids. Groaning, she rolled over and pulled the sheet over her head, but the spell of sleep had been shattered already. After a few more minutes of restless stirring, she finally gave up and threw the sheets away, swinging her legs over the side of the bed and standing.

Her sleep had been disturbed as she had been wakened throughout the night by worry after fear over Pop's condition, and the endless unanswered questions about what would come next for him. The research she had done before going to bed had been, as Mum had said it would be, contradictory and not terribly helpful.

Some of the journal literature, though, had been downright horrifying, and what sleep Katie had gotten had been punctuated by nightmares of her Pop suffering dramatic changes in his personality or intellect, and other horrors thankfully wiped away by the rising of the sun.

Katie stretched, twisting her neck one way and then the other, trying to work out the kinks of a poor night's rest, and then grabbed a pair of shorts to pull on, and flipped the sheets back into some semblance of a made bed. She could hear Gram already moving around downstairs in the kitchen, and after quickly attending to her morning routine, Katie went downstairs to join her.

"Good morning, Katydid," she said, not turning from the omelet she was preparing, as Katie came down the stairs, stepping onto the squeaky step just before they reached the bottom.

"Morning, Gram," Katie replied, still sleepy. She gave her grandmother a kiss on the cheek and said, "That looks terrific—anything I can do to help?"

"You could thaw the apple juice and mix it, if you like."

"Sure," Katie said. "No news, I assume?"

"No, nothing, but I wouldn't expect to hear anything until your father arrives tonight, and probably not even then. Your mother said they told her that it would probably take them at least a day or two to get through the initial assessments and figure out what they're looking at."

Katie looked up from reaching into the freezer for the juice and said, "Well, I guess that all we can do is hope and pray that they don't actually find anything, other than the minor injuries they know about."

She frowned as she stood up and closed the door. "Although, I guess that if Pop doesn't want me to see him, 'minor' is a relative term." She sighed and opened the cupboard for the familiar juice pitcher.

Gram turned away from the omelet, spatula in her hand. "Well, Katie, as I said, your father was never the one to come to me or Grandpa for a kiss for his boo-boos. I remember one time I found him in the bathroom, trying to tape a toenail back on that he had ripped right out somehow."

She shook her head, smiling. "It wasn't that he was ashamed to have me see him cry—in fact, it was his crying that made me come see what was going on. But he was determined to fix it himself. I still remember his tongue sticking out as he concentrated on getting the tape just right, and the lines of clean skin down his face where his tears had washed away the dirt."

Gram sighed, still smiling. "Fiercely self-reliant doesn't even begin to describe your father as a child, Katie, and his father was the same way." She gave Katie a big smile. "Come to think of it, you've got a lot of that in you, too."

Katie smiled in response as she held the frozen juice over the pitcher and waited for it to slide out of the can. "Yes, I suppose so—although I've always believed in kisses for boo-boos."

The women laughed together briefly, and then Gram remembered the omelet and turned hurriedly to check it again. Katie finished mixing the juice as Gram turned the eggs out of the pan and divided them onto plates.

They sat and ate in relative silence, each lost in thought. Most of the morning passed the same way, as Gram did her daily crossword and Katie caught up on some of the reading she was supposed to have been getting done for classes while she was away from school. Just before lunchtime, though, the phone rang, and Katie answered it.

"Hi, Mum," she said, recognizing the incoming number. "Any news?"

"Your father just changed planes in London, and he called to check in. The good news, he said, is that the medics on the flight with him seem to be less concerned than before about the blast effects. He said, too, that his hearing in that ear is starting to come back already."

"Oh, that's great news, Mum! Anything else?"

"Well, they are pretty sure now that his shoulder is bad. How bad they won't know until they can do X-rays, CAT scans and so on, but he said that they told him not to expect that he'll be able to go back soon, if ever."

"Oh, wow," Katie said. "So, what does that mean?"

"Well, it means that your father will just have to live with staying here in the States for a while, probably, and I might actually get to see what his face looks like for a while," her Mum said, her voice a mixture of humor and seriousness.

"Of course, it also means that he probably won't be able to grab that early retirement that he was hoping for. I can't say that I'm too upset about that, though—I'd rather have him here working, in one piece, than somewhere else chasing a retirement that you and I both know he'd probably never actually take anyway."

Katie nodded thoughtfully. "Yes, I have to admit that the thought of seeing Pop actually retire seems improbable. I don't suppose that there's any insurance for this sort of thing?"

"No, but the firm is generally pretty good about taking care of its own under these circumstances."

"Okay, that's good to hear. Although, Mum, you know, I can take a job to take on some more of the financial load for school."

"No, Katie, you just worry about getting the grades you'll need to get into the program you want. Your father and I are both incredibly proud of what you've done so far, and we're both looking forward to seeing you graduate and start your practice."

"Thanks, Mum," Katie said, nodding and smiling into the phone. "I don't think that I told you yet, but I'm thinking pretty seriously about setting up here. I can be closer to Gram, then, so I can probably even help her out if she needs me to."

Katie held her breath until her mother replied, "Oh, Katie, that sounds like a wonderful idea! I know how close you are to Gram, and I love the idea of you being there to give her a hand. I'm sure that your father will be thrilled to hear that, too."

"Well, also, with this newspaper that we found here, she's not going to have any trouble staying in the house now, unless something really awful and unexpected happens, like it turns out to be some sort of a hoax."

"From what you've said, that seems pretty unlikely, Katie."

"Yes, I'm feeling pretty confident about that. Oh, did you hear about that awful man from up North, who basically accused me, on-camera, of having put the thing together as a fraud?"

"What? No! Does he have anything to base this on?"

"No, Mum, nothing. George says that the guy has a history of making unfounded accusations like this, for the publicity."

"That sounds like all too many people I've known," her mother replied with a sigh.

Katie smiled into the phone, "Yes, Mum. Okay, well, I want to tell Gram the good news, okay?"

"Sure," her mother said, "I'll keep you posted as I know anything new."

"Thanks, Mum—and please, if he's up to it, can you have Pop call when he gets in tonight? I want to talk to him myself. I'll bring the phone up to my room, so he can call anytime, okay?"

"I'll see what we can do, Katie. It will depend a lot on what the medical folks want to do with him, you know?"

"Yeah, I understand," Katie said. "But try, okay?"

"I will," her mother promised. "Give my love to Gram, and

take care."

"Will do, Mum. Bye!"

"Goodbye, dear."

Katie put the phone down and went into the living room, where Gram had fallen asleep over her crossword. As Katie walked in, though, her grandmother awoke with a jump and looked up smiling sheepishly.

"I guess I didn't get very much sleep last night," she admitted to Katie.

"Yeah, me neither," Katie smiled. "I just spoke to Mum."

Gram sat up straight and said, "Oh?"

"Yeah, she heard from Pop while he changed planes in London. Sounds like he's maybe not hurt as badly as they had feared, at least with that brain trauma that you mentioned, which is a relief. The shoulder, though, may be at least temporarily disabling so things are kind of in flux as far as his job goes, I guess."

"Well, we'll worry about that after we know that his head is okay."

"I'm not going to worry about it at all, Gram. I'm sure that everything will work out okay as far as that's concerned. Right now, though"—Katie was surprised to find her eyes suddenly filling with tears—"I just want my Pop back."

"I know, child, and I want my little boy back in one piece too." Katie nodded, wiping away her tears, and went to Gram's side, embracing her tightly as they both cried silently.

# Chapter 24

Harold Gauthier's appearance on the road in front of the Harris farm was neither welcome nor unexpected. His news, however, was surprising in its grimness.

"Charles Town is besieged," he told Justin bluntly, gratefully sipping at the cup of hot tea Elizabeth had offered him. "The British have entirely encircled the city, with at least ten thousand men. Clinton holds the harbor. What is more, the pox have been reported in the town, so I cannot in good conscience even urge you to go to its defense. Never mind that you have family who will probably be on the opposing lines."

As Gauthier slurped at his tea and looked shrewdly at Justin over the rim of his cup, Justin thought furiously. His would not be an easy decision under any circumstances. Clearly, the situation was dire, and perhaps even hopeless. Justin's breakdown upon returning from action before was receding into memory now, but he knew that the same forces still raged within his heart even now.

And, what Gauthier said about his family on the opposing lines was probably not without merit. From what Terrance had found in trying to track down his family and friends from Jeremiah's plantation, the Harris family had, by and large, slipped out of view, but were widely known to be supplying intelligence and support of various sorts to the British forces that had harried and feinted at Charles Town and its surrounds for the past few years.

With British ascendancy clearly on the horizon, Justin knew that they would resume what they viewed as their rightful position at the side of their King's men. Finally, Elizabeth's protruding belly provided the final argument that Justin needed to know his mind clearly.

Reluctantly, he said, "I... have given what I can already for this cause, Harold. Even now, I accept the Continental and South-Carolina notes in lieu of specie for my crop, and hardly anyone else will accept them in turn. My farm, which ought to be prosperous, is barely hanging on. I should be building a new house this year for Elizabeth and the children to live in, and I cannot do that."

Justin's voice broke a bit as he continued, "Harold, I know what the British will do, should Charles Town fall. I remember what they did last year in Savannah. For the first time since Sullivan's Island, I truly fear for our safety on this farm—but I do not see how I can ensure that in any way by leaving to go and join the Georgia regiment rotting in British prison ships!"

Gauthier said nothing, but nodded and tossed back the last of the tea. "I understand completely, Justin. In truth, had you said that you wanted to ride for Charles Town, I was prepared to try to talk you out of it, for just those reasons."

He stood and sighed. "No, the real reason for my visit today, Justin, was to say my farewell and wish you luck in the dark days that I fear are to come. If, by some miracle, God smiles on Charles Town a second time and we are spared, I will see you again soon. Otherwise, you must do what you need to in order to keep your family safe." He gave Justin an intense, significant stare. "Whatever you need to, Justin." He motioned with his chin at Elizabeth's belly. "Keep them safe."

"Thank you, my friend," Justin said, and stood to embrace the older man. "May God bless and keep you, Harold. I'll see you soon."

Gauthier nodded to the others at the table. "Elizabeth, Terrance, take care." He squared his shoulders, looking around the tidy house, dimly lit and warmed by the fireplace, windows shuttered against the chilly breeze, the older children working on their daytime chores in the corner, and he smiled grimly. "Take care of them all, Justin." He donned his hat and pulled his heavy cloak tight around him and then went outside, closing the door firmly behind him.

# Chapter 25

Katie sat propped on a giant stuffed panda Grandpa had won for her at the county fair many years ago, reading a textbook that was failing utterly to keep her attention. How could she keep her thoughts focused on the role of changes in the textile industry as contributing factors in the War Between the States, when her Pop was returning to the States, battered and possibly seriously injured?

Still, she struggled on, because the alternative was to lie down and surrender herself to the nightmares of the unknown. The phone blinked its readiness on the bedside table beside her, and she glared at it, willing it to ring. The phone sat mute, however, and Katie forced herself to read another paragraph, another page of turgid prose describing the natural decline of the institution of slavery in the face of increasing mechanization and the advent of the steam-powered—

And then the phone did ring, and Katie snatched it up before the first ring had even finished, answering breathlessly, "Hello?"

"Hi, Katie," she heard her Pop's voice, sounding thick and slow.

"Hi, Pop," she said, tears instantly pouring down her cheeks. "How are you feeling?"

"Well, I've felt better, I won't lie," he answered. "They'll know more tomorrow, but they say that I probably got lucky and managed to avoid permanent injury."

"Oh, Pop," Katie said, sniffling despite herself. "I was so scared."

"I know, Honey," he said. "And I want you to know, too, that I had a lot of time to think about everything on the way home. I have decided that I'm not going back, even if they can patch me all up."

She heard him pause and blow his nose, and fresh tears welled into her eyes at the thought of her Pop crying. He continued, "I'll help out the firm Stateside, if they'll have me, but I'm staying here from now on. I watched my driver, a man I'd sat beside for the past five months, who had three small children and a wife all depending on him completely—I watched them roll the truck off of his body, after they got me out. Just like that—pfft—everything that he was trying to do for his family was gone, over."

He blew his nose again. "Katie, I want to be here and watch you finish with school and fall in love and have kids of your own, and I want to roll around on the floor with them and amaze them with stories about what it was like to watch Neil Armstrong step onto the Moon, and see you succeeding as a great doctor, and—well, all of that, Katie. I realized that I've been making my choices based on some false premises, and that one of those was that I could be there for you, no matter where I was. I realized that my place is here, and I want to stay."

"Oh, Pop," Katie repeated, "I'm just so glad that you're home, and I'm glad that you're staying. I've been scared for you all the time, though I haven't said anything, because you seemed so happy with your work."

"I love what I was doing, and it needs to be done, very

badly. Those people over there are counting on men like me to get the job done. But frankly, my obligations, my responsibilities, are here. We'll make it all work, all of the details. For now, though, I just wanted to tell you what I told your Mum—I'm back, and I'm staying."

"Okay, Pop. I'm glad to hear it, and yes, we'll make it all work. Right now, though, you let them take care of you, okay?"

"You bet, Sunshine. I think that they'll have me presentable in a few days, and then maybe you can come up, or maybe I'll even be in good enough shape to come on down there and see you and Gram both, in a week or so."

"Oh, that would be wonderful, Pop. I know that Gram would be awfully happy to see you, too."

"Well, I'll see what they are willing to let me do, once they've had a chance to run me through all of their scanners and whatnot up here, okay?"

"Sounds good, Pop. You take care—I can't wait to see you."

He chuckled painfully. "Well, you can wait for a few days, sweetie. They've got to get my face put back together first. I caught a lot of glass and debris with the side of my head, I guess, so they've got to get that all cleaned out, and the medics said that it'll only look worse before it looks better."

"Okay, Pop. I'll try to be patient. But you know that I don't care what you look like—you're still my Pop."

"Yes, sweetie, but I care, so we'll wait for a little while longer."

"All right, Pop. Get some rest."

"You, too, and let Gram know that I'm going to be okay."

"Will do, Pop. Good night."

"G'night, Sunshine."

Katie hung up the phone and put it down, using the sleeve of her t-shirt to wipe her eyes before she marked her place in her book and set it next to the phone and turned off the light. She was asleep within minutes, and she slept soundly until the sun tickled her eyelashes again the next morning.

# Chapter 26

"You are Justin Harris?" The constable was not really asking, so much as stating a known fact. "And this is your wife Elizabeth, and your negro Terrance. Good, then, let's get on with this." The short, officious man, his balding head shining with the heat of the early summer day drew out a sheaf of papers and thrust the top one at Justin.

"You will sign this declaration of your personal allegiance to and support of His Majesty, King George the Third. If you cannot sign your name, please make your mark and I will witness it." Justin looked at the page that awaited his signature. He took up the quill and with outward calm, but a raging heart, dipped it into the inkpot and signed his name in full.

The constable nodded, seeming almost disappointed that Justin had not put up a fight. He presented the next paper to Justin. "Now we come to the matter of the negro. Your cousin's widow Anna has filed a claim on the negro known as 'Terrance,' who was loaned to you before the troubles that included the murder of her husband. She states here that you took advantage of the confusion surrounding those events to make permanent your possession of the negro—"

"That's a lie!" Justin could not restrain his fury. "I have a proper bill of sale from my late cousin, and furthermore, I have manumitted Terrance, and he is a free man, not a chattel property."

"Ah, yes, she did say that you had deluded the poor creature into believing that he was a freeman, but she produced adequate proofs of her claim to the Crown Court in Charles Town, and they have issued this full and proper writ commanding you to return the negro to her estate."

The little man looked to his left, where an armed dragoon stood. "We are empowered to enforce this writ, by force if necessary. The negro comes with us." He nodded to the soldier, who moved with surprising speed for his size, stepping behind Terrance and grabbing his arm, before he even had a chance to start for the door.

Terrance's features, which had until now been impassive and then shocked, now sagged with resignation. "It's all right, Mister Harris," he said, his deep voice sad but calm. "There's nothing you can do about it right now, but maybe you can show the court your papers and convince them that you're telling the truth, that I am a—a free man." A single tear trickled out of Terrance's eye as he stood and permitted the soldier to secure his wrists behind him with a rough length of hempen twine.

"If you can't convince them, Mister Harris, then I just want you to know that these have been the greatest years of my life, working with you here on our farm. I appreciate all that you've done for me, and I know that you'll do whatever you can now, too. Just remember what your friend told you, though. That comes first."

At that, the solider growled, "Shut up, you," and cuffed Terrance, before leading him through the door. Timothy and Katherine stood, round-eyed, disbelieving, as the enormity of the events unfolding before them sank in. Terrance nodded solemnly to both children as he left, meeting their horrified gazes with a steady expression.

"As for the rest of this lot," the constable continued, tossing the remaining papers onto the table before Justin, "you're to be permitted to continue proving this land, and your tobacco and wool will be purchased at a price to be determined by the Royal Governor, subject to your continued loyalty. We know a little bit of your history, *Corporal* Harris, and so believe me when I say that I personally think that the Governor has been exceptionally merciful in your case."

The little man straightened, gave Elizabeth a smirking half-bow, and turned, leaving the door standing open as he walked out. Justin sat, his back stiffly upright, his face frozen in a rictus of pain and rage, for several long minutes after the official and his escort had gone.

Finally, he collapsed onto the table, weeping. Elizabeth moved to sit beside him, holding his hand and stroking his hair, murmuring comfort to him.

"Papa?" Timothy asked, his voice husky and heavy. "This means that Terrance is going to be a slave again?"

Justin raise his face, his eyes closed in pain as he answered, "It means that, so far as the Crown is concerned, he always has been a slave, Timothy." He added, muttering, "As have we all."

"That's horrible, Papa! You've got to do something!"

"I will, Timothy. First thing in the morning, I'm going to leave for Charles Town to see the Crown Court and bring them my papers concerning Terrance. You should know, though, that they are unlikely to find in Terrance's favor. The court's writ is merely putting a legal finish on a kidnapping that would probably have taken place even without their blessing."

Elizabeth spoke up, "But aren't you risking even worse punishment at the Crown's hands by going before them?"

"I may be, Elizabeth... I will go, however. I owe Terrance that much, at least."

She nodded, unhappy, and took his hand to place it on her belly, now bulging with the new life that it promised. "Just don't take any unnecessary risks, all right?"

"I won't, my dear. I do remember what Harold said, God rest his soul."

The next morning, he saddled up the mare himself for the first time in years, realizing anew just how much he had depended on Terrance, first as slave, and then as faithful friend. The tobacco plants stood in the early light, their crowns dipping with the weight of the morning dew. Justin knew that if his attempt to win Terrance's freedom failed, he would have to reduce the fields to what he and Timothy could manage.

He shook his head angrily, dismissing the thought, and spurred the mare onto the road, making for town and beyond.

# Chapter 27

Walking stiffly out of the terminal on his wife's arm, Pop spotted Katie and Gram before they recognized him. Katie rushed to them, holding him tightly and blocking the exit for a moment. Gram waited for her turn, and then embraced her son no less ardently, as Katie held her mother. All of them were weeping openly.

Passers-by looked curiously at the wounded man before politely turning their gazes away. The right side of his head was shaved back to the midline of his scalp, and dozens of angry pink welts of scar tissue spread over the exposed skin. Several extended around to his face, and his eye was still swollen shut on that side, as well.

When Katie was able to speak, she observed wryly, "Well, Pop, you were right—you're a mess. But I'm awfully glad to see you, anyway."

Gram added, "Joe, you've really done it this time, haven't you? "

"Well, I had some help, Ma. They would have done worse, had they been able."

"I know, Son. I know. I'm very, very glad to see you again. Let's get you home, okay?"

"Yes, Ma, that sounds good. Kim, do you mind if I just go to the car with Ma while you and Katie get our bags?"

His wife kissed him on the cheek, her eyes still shining with tears. "No problem, Joe. I'll see you in a minute, okay?"

The four split into two pairs and headed off in their separate directions.

After Gram and Pop were out of earshot, Katie said, "Mum?"

"Yes, Katie?"

"Did they say anything about the scarring? Will they be able to make him look... like he did before?"

"They said that things will need to heal a bit before they can begin the reconstructive surgery, but yes, he will look like your Pop again."

"Okay," Katie said, "I hope I don't sound too horrible, asking that. It was just... shocking."

"I know, Katie. But he's going to be okay. Everything's going to be okay." She took a deep, shuddering breath, her tears starting up again. "It's all going to be okay," she repeated. Katie hugged her mother close, and after several moments, they separated, nodding to each other and smiling.

"I know, Mum. Thanks for coming. The bag claim is down this way now—they've re-arranged everything again, of course."

Busying herself with the details of finding the right baggage carousel, Katie was able to stop thinking about how ghastly her Pop had actually looked, and how haggard and grey Mum was looking, for her part.

# Chapter 28

Justin had grown accustomed to the relatively constant smell of smoke as he journeyed toward Charles Town. Loyalists and British troops alike had acted to punish many participants in the rebellion against the King, and the smoldering ruins of houses and estates had punctuated the entire trip.

There were also other signs of the fresh British victory in the Colony. The pennants flying from the government house where his tobacco would be bound in just a few short months were again all the Crown's, rather than the jaunty Continental standards. At several points along the way, Justin was obliged to stand aside for squads of troops moving about the countryside, going about the business of maintaining control over a recently rebellious land.

Most of all, though, Justin noted that the mood of the people in the hamlets he passed through, and at the inn that he normally stayed in at the end of the first day's travel, were subdued, resigned, much as Justin himself was. The loyalists among them, of course, ranged anywhere from outright jubilation to grim satisfaction at seeing a longtime wrong at last set to rights.

The second night, though, the tavern at the inn was buzzing angrily—except when a British patrol stepped in briefly, but the muttered curses and stories resumed as soon as the patrol was gone again. News had just arrived of a skirmish in the north of the state, where a British colonel had been pursuing a small troop of

Virginian soldiers.

The man who had brought the news was surrounded by a crowd of colonists, who took in his account with growing disbelief and anger. He was unkempt and looked as though he had neither shaved nor rested in days.

The man growled, "This British colonel, may his mother never stop weeping, he saw the flag of truce, took note of it, and had one of his men shoot down the drummer carrying it. The Virginians had already laid down arms, and when they saw their truce flag fall, they took up their rifles again—but it was too late."

The ragged man took a deep draught of his mug and shook his head. "When the charge was done, the American militia lay dead or wounded almost to a man. The British advanced upon them and used bayonets to dispatch the living, and to commit horrors on the corpses of the dead for their own entertainments." He shuddered.

"I went to the field of the battle to see what I could do to help give peace to the souls lost there. I saw carnage unlike any I could ha' previous imagined. That men could do this to other men—" He stopped and drained his cup.

"I found one man whom I first took to be among the dead—he was thrust through with bayonet no less than four times, never mind the shot that first knocked him down. He told me what he had seen as my wife tended to his wounds. I do not know if he will recover, but I came to seek aid for him and to speak with the colonel's commanding officer myself, if I can."

The savagery of the British action was shocking to nearly all who heard it, even in the face of the recent plunder of Charles Town. A local man said, his voice low and angry, "It's one thing for soldiers to succumb to the temptations of a prostrate city before them, filled with the rich goods of active trade at its capture. I don't like it, but I can understand and forgive, to a point."

He chuckled roughly, "Though the British aren't making any friends hereabouts, either, stealing from both Patriot and Loyalist alike, and taking nearly everything of value from some places. Silverware, tools, horses, stores—they took everything that wasn't nailed down, even slaves. How they expect us to go on making a living is beyond my ken."

Another man spoke up, his voice quavering, "I know of insults done to ladies at a number of plantations and farms in the area, and not by irregulars or vengeful Tories—these were regular British troops, supposedly civilized and well-ordered." The man shook his head, his expression bleak, and returned to his cup. Justin finished his supper and retired to his room, reflecting on what he'd heard.

The sense of quiet, desperate resignation that Justin had seen elsewhere in his journey was replaced by something less settled, more dangerous. Justin had the sense that he was advancing ever deeper into a powder keg with a fuse alight.

As he rode into Charles Town the next day, he was shocked at the changes to the place he'd known for so many years. Earthworks were thrown up all around the approach to the town, and a tremendous crater marked the explosion of some storehouse or battery outside the walls. The pennant of the conqueror flew everywhere over the city, and the stars and stripes and other American banners had vanished.

Nearly every house bore the signs of bombardment, fire, or both. The familiar spire of the church at the center of town was blackened—he learned when he inquired that this was actually done by the defenders to make it less prominent—and the pall of smoke in his nose was overpowering. In places, it was the sharp smell of gunpowder; in others areas, less savory odors mingled to present a horrifying blend.

Easier, Justin thought grimly, to come upon a city he had not known and find it in such condition, than to see this destruction visited upon a place he had known for so long. As he passed through the streets, he noted that the town dwellings of the members of his own family had not been spared, either. His uncle's home lay in ashes, only the stone chimney rising from the ruin, and the home where Justin had grown up, since passed to a cousin, had apparently been hit directly by cannon shot, evidently several times. Not even the chimney stood upon that lot.

Justin made his way to the State House where, he presumed, the Crown magistrate would be. Tying his mare up outside, he joined the crowd jostling its way in and out of the building, clutching the satchel of papers that would, in a just world, restore Terrance's freedom. However, Justin was not certain that he lived in a just world any longer.

Eventually, after telling his tale what seemed like a dozen times, he was ushered into the magistrate's chambers, where he was shocked to recognize an old friend of his father's under the powdered wig and robes of the office. The old man motioned Justin to approach.

"Justin Harris," he said, his voice completely lacking the warmth once heard there. "I was told that you might make an appearance on the behalf of that negro of your cousin's. I will remind you, before you begin, that you are suffered to appear here under parole, based on your actions in opposition to the Crown's troops as they rightfully attempted to return Charles Town and South-Carolina to His Majesty's good graces four years ago."

Justin swallowed hard. "I am aware of the terms of the capitulation to the Crown, your honor. I do not challenge any part of the parole I subscribed to just these four days past. As you anticipated, I seek only to right a terrible wrong that has been done to the negro free man, Terrance."

He hurried on, presenting the documents from his satchel as he spoke. "I have here the original sales agreement between myself and my late, lamented cousin Jeremiah. Here, the completed bill of sale, recording satisfactory performance on my part of the contract of payment. It is all in order, and bears all of the proper witnesses and seals. And here, I have the manumission that I executed for my slave, in recognition of extraordinary services rendered to me and to my family. Again, all properly recorded and witnessed."

Justin stood, his heart pounding in his throat, as the magistrate examined each of the documents, his face expressionless as he did so. The chamber was close and hot in the rising heat of the day, and the all-pervasive smell of smoke left Justin feeling slightly nauseated on top of everything else.

"Well, Mister Harris," the magistrate finally said, still betraying no hint of friendship, "I am forced to agree that these documents do appear to be all in order, and that the facts of the matter are as you represented them."

Justin felt tears of relief spring to his eyes, and remembered to breathe for the first time since passing the documents over.

The magistrate continued, "However, I am sorry to inform you that the negro Terrance was consigned upon his arrival in Charles Town yesterday to the transport Huron, which has weighed anchor for Barbados with this morning's tide. Much as I would like to set right this miscarriage of justice, he is beyond my reach at this time."

Justin closed his eyes and willed himself to continue breathing, as he felt the blood drain out of his face. "Barbados," he whispered at last. "Whatever did that poor creature do to deserve such a fate?"

"Your cousin's widow would answer for her false witness before this court, save that she has, herself, also this very morning departed this country, returning home to England. She, too, is now beyond the reach of this court, nor is she likely to be returned for even such cause as this, under the circumstances."

The magistrate sighed deeply. "I am sorry, Mister Harris, but there is nothing further that I can do for you or for the free negro Terrance. I will confess to you that when the widow brought this action before me last week, I gave the matter little thought, given the state of the country at the time that she alleged you took the negro as your own. I owe you an apology for that presumption, but there seemed little to doubt in her claim."

Justin held his tongue, his face flaming now, his rage again rising on behalf of his faithful friend, who had been so roughly served by the events over which he had had no control and in which he had played no part but a beneficial one.

Finally, when he could trust himself to speak, he said only, "Thank you for your trouble, your honor," then turned and left this place of supposed justice behind.

# Chapter 29

As Mum was getting Pop settled into the guest room—the same room he'd slept in as a boy—Katie poured iced tea for herself and Gram downstairs in the kitchen.

Katie commented, "Must be rough, changing time zones that quickly. It's what, almost midnight over there? I'd want a nap, too!"

"I never could keep up with the right time over there. When he took the job, I kept a small clock by the phone at first, but since I could never seem to catch him at a convenient time, I just started waiting for him to call instead." She shrugged. "At least he's home now, and here to stay."

Katie nodded and took a long, thirsty drink of her tea.

Her mother came downstairs, and Katie smiled, "Hi, Mum! So, was he asleep before you left the room?"

Mum sat down at the kitchen table and smiled back, "Yes, pretty much. Long flight, and he's had a long few days here, too."

Katie stood up to refill her iced tea, asking, "Did you want some tea, too, Mum?"

"Sure, Katie, that sounds nice, thanks."

Just as Katie was fetching another glass from the cupboard, the phone rang. "I'll get it," she said, and grabbed it. "Harris residence, Katie Harris speaking."

"Hi, Katie! I've got great news," said George, sounding

barely able to contain himself.

"Oh? What's up?"

"I'm sitting here with Professor Schulmann, who has examined the issue of the *Mercury* that we found in your grandmother's house, and he is now in agreement that it is a genuine document, and that the text of the Mecklenburg Declaration printed on it is also genuine."

"Whoa, wow! How did this all happen?"

"Well, out of an abundance of academic rigor, I issued an invitation to him to inspect the document for himself, along with the evidence of its provenance. Of course, given his public statements, I did not expect him to accept, but I thought that it was good form to extend the olive branch anyhow."

George chuckled a little and continued, "I don't think that Larry—sorry, Professor Schulmann—actually anticipated that I would invite him to look at the thing, either, but he couldn't resist the opportunity to satisfy himself that he was right to accuse us of a hoax."

"So, what convinced him, anyway?"

"Well, his suspicion was mostly due to the fact that I went to the media so quickly, and, of course, there is a history of hoaxes and forgeries around this particular document, so that raised his concern as well. Once he saw the thing for himself, and heard my account of the circumstances under which we found it, he realized that his initial reaction was overly skeptical."

"Not to mention vicious and mean," Katie interjected, remembering what he had said about her, personally.

"Yes, he would like to apologize to you for that, Katie. May I put him on?"

"Uh, sure, I guess."

"Okay, just a second."

Katie heard the phone being passed to the other man, and then heard his noxious accent, but with a warmer tone now. "Good afternoon, Miss Harris. Lawrence Schulmann here. I do owe you a sincere apology. I was out of line in my comments, and I'm willing to say so, publicly, if you like."

Katie replied coldly, "Professor Schulmann, I'm glad that you figured out that you made a mistake, but you have to know that you could have really hurt me, academically. What you said was mean-spirited and wrong, and, frankly, irresponsible." Katie found that she was shaking slightly as she rebuked the man.

She heard him take a deep breath of resignation before he replied. "I know that, Miss Harris. You must understand though, that in my decades in this field of study, I have penetrated any number of hoaxes. I had every reason to believe that you were just another fortune-seeker with a knack for digital manipulation."

The nasal accent became more pronounced as he spoke, and Katie found herself getting angry all over again. "I'll be honest with you, Professor Schulmann. I want to ensure that you think twice before attacking someone else. I'm told that you have a history of making baseless accusations whenever you think you've found a hoax, and I'd really hope that you would change your basic attitude of mistrust."

By the time she was done speaking, she realized that her voice had become shrill, and she waited, breathing hard, for his reply. Finally, he spoke, softly. "I will try to be more mindful in the future, Miss Harris. I made a mistake, and I know—my colleagues never tire of telling me—that I tend to express myself in obnoxious ways." He sighed. "I'm not going to bore you with the details of my life, Miss Harris, but suffice to say that I am aware of that flaw in my personality, and I try to rein it in."

His own tone had become less warm, and he said, abruptly, "I'll let you speak to Professor Branton again now."

George's voice returned to the phone now, "Okay, Katie, so are you reasonably satisfied, then?"

"Yes, I suppose so," Katie said, a bit reluctantly. "If you can say so, why is he suddenly so eager to make nice, anyway?"

"I think, Katie," George said quietly, "that he got scared of damaging his reputation further when he realized what we were actually looking at. He's not a bad man, just perhaps a bit quick to draw conclusions sometimes. And, as he said, he's working on that tendency within himself."

"Well, I guess I'm glad to hear that, but I wish that he'd worked on it a bit more before he came out swinging after me," Katie said.

"I don't disagree one bit. Hey, how's your father doing?"

"Well, we just picked him up at the airport, and he's napping at the moment. Between some leftover jet lag, and being hurt and then traveling, he was pretty bushed. He looks... well, he looks rough, but that will heal, over time. Thanks for asking, George."

"No problem—tell him I said hi, when he wakes up, okay?"

"Sure thing, George. Thanks for calling."

"You're welcome, Katie. Talk to you later."

Katie hung up the phone and put it back into the base, then stared for a moment at the empty glass in her hand. She shook herself, remembering why she had gone into the kitchen in the first place, and poured the iced tea for herself and her Mum.

# Chapter 30

As he wearily rode over the rise to where he could see his fields, Justin was gratified to note that Timothy was out plucking the under leaves from the tobacco plants. He sighed and wondered whether he shouldn't try to keep the additional fields up with Timothy taking up some of what Terrance once had done. The boy was strong, and was a fast study. Perhaps, perhaps...

The taverns all the way back from Charles Town had been full of angry talk about the British outrages as they reasserted their dominion over the Colony. Justin could not bring himself to feel the hatred he'd heard against the British, though. The rebellion was clearly faltering throughout the Colonies, and it seemed to Justin that continuing to stir trouble was simply counterproductive.

Justin rode down to the house, taking his time with the tack and wiping down the mare, before he turned her out to graze at her leisure. He felt no eagerness to share the news of what he had learned in Charles Town, nor of the conditions he'd seen there.

Finally, though, he drew a great, gusty sigh and went inside the house, where Elizabeth sat, teaching Katherine to spin. The girl's movements were already smooth and practiced, if not as speedy as her mother's, and Justin took a moment to simply appreciate the industriousness of his family, even under the circumstances of sadness and worry.

"Hello, Elizabeth," he eventually said, and she nodded, still counting under her breath.

"Hello, Justin," she interjected as she turned the spindle. "I'll be done here in a moment."

Justin nodded in reply and looked at her in the dim light of the windows and flickering fire. Her face was aglow with exertion and the warmth of the summer day, but her beauty was all the greater for it. She sat awkwardly, twisted half around to work past the baby in her womb, but seemed mindless of the discomfort.

She looked up at him and smiled at seeing him gazing raptly at her. There was sadness in her eyes, too as she said, "I can see from your face, Justin, that you haven't any good news about Terrance."

He nodded sadly. "No, I have not. My cousin's widow Anna bore false witness before the magistrate, sold Terrance into bondage on British Barbados, and then fled with the proceeds. I am afraid that justice will have to wait for God's time, for she seems to have evaded any justice in this life."

Elizabeth closed her eyes tightly as she absorbed the news of Terrance's fate, and then nodded in agreement. "God will not judge her kindly, I am sure. Though perhaps this, too, is all part of His plan. Did not Terrance say that his son had been sold from his plantation in Georgia into service on that same island?"

"Indeed, I believe you are correct, Elizabeth. It may be His will that Terrance be reunited with his kin, and that the ties of blood are more important in His plan than matters of freedom or bondage." Justin sighed again. "Though," he said sadly, "I am not sure that any of us will find much freedom here, either."

"I know, Justin. The widow Prescott was by to check on me in your absence, and she related to me some of the tales that are making their way through the Colony. We may yet yearn for the day when we were merely taxed without our consent."

Justin gave a brief bark of laughter. "Oh, but that is the one thing that the Crown has declared that it will cede—we will only suffer such taxation as we are willing to vote for ourselves. So, in all of this, we have at least won that right."

Elizabeth nodded her head, wearily. "It seems a great deal to have endured for so little gain," she said, after a moment. "Still, it is good to hear that all of our sacrifices have not been completely in vain."

"I only hope that this war can be brought to a reasonable conclusion across the Colonies, without any further atrocities," said Justin. "His Majesty risks sparking a new rebellion if he cannot bring his forces into line with civilized conduct."

"That is His Majesty's burden to bear, Justin. Ours is to make the best of our circumstance. I think that Timothy would step into Terrance's place at your side, to the extent that he can."

"I thought the same, Elizabeth, when I saw him tending to the tobacco as I rode in." He nodded. "I am sure that we will do fine, so long as tranquility returns soon, and is maintained. Indeed," he said, remembering the scenes of destruction he had witnessed in Charles Town, "we are in better condition than some in this Colony, and we have much to be thankful for."

Katherine spoke up now, "I do so wish that Terrance were back home with you, Papa. Will he perhaps escape from Barbados once he is reunited with his son?"

Justin sighed, "I doubt it very much, Katherine, dear, but if it is God's will, then we will have a place ready for Terrance upon his return, I promise you that."

Katherine thought about it, her expression sober. "I'll make sure that his lambs are tended," she said. "So he will have something to make him happy when he comes home."

"I'm certain that Terrance would like that, Katherine," Justin said.

# Chapter 31

Once again, Katie listened to Gram invoke the old prayer as they sat at the dinner table. "*Komm, Herr Jesu, sei unser Gast Und segne, was Du uns bescheret hast.*" This time, though, there was a full chorus of "amen" at the end, with her Mum and Pop's voices joining in. She raised her head and opened her eyes, smiling at the full table.

Her mother said, "Pass the rolls, please, dear?"

"Sure thing," Katie said, grinning. "I helped Gram with these," she said, as proud as if she were still a little girl in her child-sized apron.

"Well, I'm glad to hear that somebody's learning Gram's kitchen secrets," Pop said, good-naturedly. "Your Aunt Lily certainly never had any interest in cooking."

"Now, Joe, you can't fault her for that. You two were both too occupied with figuring out how to take the house apart to ever have much interest in that," Gram rejoined, her own face alight with a smile the likes of which Katie hadn't seen since she arrived for this visit.

"True enough, Ma," he said. "I remember one time that she showed me how to take the handles off of the faucets. Pa wasn't real amused, though." He chuckled at the memory.

"Oh, so that's what happened?" Gram laughed. "We were completely baffled at how she got those taken off while she was over at her friend's house!"

Pop laughed along with her, and then closed his eyes, smiling peacefully. "I had forgotten how nice it is to just sit around the table with family, instead of catching meals wherever I happen to be, eating in the company of people who I don't care at all about."

He shook his head. "I am so thankful to be here, to have had the opportunities I've had, and to have all of you to return to. No, I am not going back, nor am I going to go anywhere else that keeps me from sitting down to dinner with you, Kim."

His wife gazed back at him as he opened his eyes to look at her. Katie understood, in a flash of insight, just how much sacrifice had been involved in his work—and how much was involved in changing to a different path now.

"Thank you, Pop," she said quietly. "Thank you for coming home. You will find a way to continue to help those folks from here, I'm sure... but I'm glad that you're staying here."

"Oh, Katie, I cannot imagine doing anything differently," he said. "I'm glad I went, I'm glad I did the work that I did—and I'm glad that I made it back. I'm not going to tempt fate further. I think that Somebody was giving me a tap on the shoulder to remind me of what is truly important in my life."

He looked around the table again. "And this is it."

# Chapter 32

Hannah Prescott held Elizabeth's hand. "Okay, I can see the baby's head, Elizabeth! It's time to push now. Just hold my hand and push, honey!" Elizabeth drew a deep breath and strained, the tendons in her neck standing out and sweat pouring down her red face. The wail that was ripped from her throat tore at Justin's ears where he waited on the other side of the room with the children.

When her cry faded, though, a new one rose in the silence, thin and fitful. Hannah called out, "It's a boy!" and lifted the baby to his mother's breast. Justin gripped his elder children's hands tightly as tears of joy sprang to his eyes.

"A son," he murmured. "William Harris. William Terrance Harris."

Once the afterbirth was done, and Hannah had cleaned up Elizabeth and the baby, she called Justin and the children over. Elizabeth looked tired but, to Justin's eyes, more beautiful than ever, as she cradled the swaddled baby in her arms. William slept at his mother's breast, a shock of hair protruding from under the blanket wrapped around the crown of his head.

"He's beautiful, Elizabeth," Justin said. He took a deep breath, and looked upward, giving thanks to the Maker for the blessings of this day. He gave thanks, too, for the chance, denied to so many of late, to enjoy those blessings with his family. He felt, for the first time in years, at peace.

# Chapter 33

Doctor Kate Harris walked out onto the veranda with a fresh glass of iced tea and sat down in the creaky old rocking chair, the noise startling her grandmother from her snooze.

"Sorry about that, Gram," she said, as she settled into the chair and sipped at her tea.

"Oh, don't worry about it, Katie," she replied, shading her eyes from the slanting rays of the late-afternoon sun. "I'm just tuckered out after your parents' visit."

Kate smiled, nodding. "I know what you mean. It's as if he wants to make sure that we do all the things that he feels like he missed, being over there for so long. I appreciate it, but I agree, their visits can be exhausting."

Pointing at the still-glistening paint on simple turned spindles lining the edge of the veranda, she continued, "At least the railing's all fixed up now, and he got that beautiful reproduction of the newspaper hung up for you."

In due course, the copy of the *Cape Fear Mercury* had been authenticated and went to auction. It had been a pleasant surprise when the buyer, a high-tech executive from Raleigh, had arranged to have museum-quality copies made for both Gram and for George Branton. Gram's had been delivered last week in a nice frame, but they hadn't gotten around to hanging it yet when Kate's parents arrived.

Gram nodded, her eyes sliding closed again, and a contented smile on her face. Kate sighed and rocked slightly, taking another sip of her iced tea. The cooling evening air was like a velvet blanket on her face, and she hoped that the sense of well-being that she felt in this moment would last the rest of her life.

# Epilogue

A peaceful reunion with Great Britain was not the fate of South-Carolina, nor the rest of the Colonies. British rule continued to be harsh and capricious, motivating a fresh wave of rebellion across South-Carolina. With fresh resolve, the rebels in the South and throughout the Colonies successfully won their independence, and South-Carolina was only freed from the burden of British occupation in the waning days of the war.

Justin and his family remained relatively unmolested throughout the balance of the war, although their town saw heavy action at one point along the way. The elder Harris children insisted on maintaining Terrance's share of the farm themselves, and prevailed upon Justin to set aside the income from that portion for the purpose of attempting to purchase Terrance's freedom.

After the war ended, they believed that they had accumulated sufficient capital for the project, and Justin tried to trace Terrance's fate, with the assistance of the sympathetic magistrate (now returned to private life) in Charles Town. They learned that Terrance's arrival in Barbados had come just months before a massive hurricane swept across the island. They were unsurprised to learn that Terrance had acted heroically to save his new master's children, and had been, for the second time, made a freeman.

He was eking out a living as a manual laborer on the plantation to which he had been sold, but with the money that

Justin and the children sent to him, he was able to establish himself as a builder for hire. His greatest joy, however, came when he found his son on a plantation on the other side of the island, and he gladly saved up the money necessary to purchase his freedom. Father and son worked together and were responsible for a significant portion of the slave housing built on the island for the following twenty years.

Justin's son Timothy served with distinction as an officer in the new American army, rising to the rank of major before he was felled in Lower Canada (now Québec) during the British invasion in 1812. Katherine and William both enjoyed comparatively quiet lives, remaining in South Carolina, where William inherited the farm and built the new house in which Gram lives with Kate to this day.

# *Also in Audiobook*

**M**any readers love the experience of turning the pages in a paper book such as the one you hold in your hands. Others enjoy hearing a skilled narrator tell them a tory, bringing the words on the page to life.

Brief Candle Press has arranged to have *The Declaration* roduced as a high-quality audiobook, and you can listen to a ample and learn where to purchase it in that form by scanning the QR code below with your phone, tablet, or other device, or going o the Web address shown.

Happy listening!

bit.ly/TheDeclarationAudio

# Historical Notes

**M**ost all popular histories of the American Revolution focus on the events of the northern Colonies, where indeed, many of the pivotal moments of the war and the philosophy of governance that animated the movement for independence were centered.

However, the southern Colonies were also crucial to the eventual success of the war, both because it provided crucial logistical routes to move goods for both military and civilian needs despite the forced closure of ports at Boston and New York, but also because many of the leading figures of the Revolution originated in the South.

To be sure, there was greater support for the Crown in the South than in the North, in part because of the same deeply-held cultural resistance to change that characterizes the Deep South of the modern era, and in part because of the wildly different social structure of the plantations as compared to the North's more typical smallholders. However, there was no shortage of hotheads south of the future Mason-Dixon line in the heady days leading to the outright break with England.

While no copy of it has been found (yet), the May 20, 1775 declaration by the a gathering of delegates from militia companies around Mecklenburg County, North Carolina that they were a "free and independent people" would have anticipated the

Continental Congress' Declaration of Independence by over a full year. The existence of this earlier declaration has aroused no lack of controversy over the years, including at least one fraudulent re-creation of its supposed original publication in the *Cape Fear Mercury* in June of 1775.

As it is, the well-documented Mecklenburg Resolves of May 31, 1775 were fully as radical as anything adopted in the northern Colonies, and the historical record is unambiguous about the vigor of various Committees of Correspondence, and later, well-armed Committees of Safety across the southern Colonies.

Of course, the discovery in an old family chest stashed away in the corner of some dusty attic of an authentic copy of the alleged Mecklenburg Declaration would reinvigorate the claim by proud North Carolinians of their special role in the drive toward eventual American independence.

It may be that part of the reason that our popular memory of the Revolution omits most of the events in the southern Colonies is simply that it was there that the American cause suffered its greatest defeats. With the active assistance of Loyalist forces, the British conquered and occupied most of the southern Colonies until the waning days of the war in the north.

The occupation was ungentle, even brutal at times, and the suffering of those who had stood against the Crown has received some attention in a film of recent years, but is still largely forgotten. Forced to sign loyalty oaths, dispossessed of their property (both real estate and other), and even subjected to violence at the hands of Loyalists, those who had supported the rebellion against Britain paid a high price for their convictions.

In the end, however, the rebellious Americans prevailed,

and between the efforts of the well-known "Swamp Fox" General Marion and the pivotal battle at Cowpens, they ejected the British from the south, driving them northward to their ultimate defeat at Yorktown.

The heroic efforts of the Patriots of the southern Colonies have long been overdue for greater recognition, and I am glad to do some small part toward that in telling the story of some of the people who made huge sacrifices and achieved stunning victories in our movement from subjects of the Crown to citizens of the Republic.

# Acknowledgements

I am deeply grateful to my friends Matthew Blackstone and Cassie Myers Jamison, whose comments to me about the importance of the Carolinas in the Revolution spurred me to learn more—and ultimately, to tell at least one of the stories of that time and place. Matthew also helped me to locate the events of the story in a place that matched my prose much more closely than where I had originally envisioned, adding greatly to the verisimilitude of the novel's sense of place.

I would also like to gratefully acknowledge the assistance of my fellow novelist of the Revolution, Michelle Isenhoff, who very kindly not only looked over the manuscript for this book, but also provided invaluable suggestions and edits to it, greatly improving it.

Innumerable researchers and writers of the Revolutionary era provided details that I dropped into this story, hopefully unobtrusively, adding to its realism and value as a means of better understanding the Revolution.

Again, I wish to acknowledge the good people at the National Novel Writing Month program, whose structure, support and cheerleading gave me the tools to take on this project in the first place. After arriving at the wrong location to join my writing group, locking myself out of my car, walking ten miles home in the middle of the night, being given a short ride by a kind police officer (yes, in the barred, uncomfortable back seat of his cruiser), and still gritting my way through the first few thousand words before going to bed, I knew that there was no way that I could let any smaller obstacle prevent me from pressing forward to completing this novel.

Finally, I want to thank every one of my readers, who have provided me with more support, thoughtful criticism, and inspiration than I ever could have anticipated when I first sat down to write. You are, truly, the reason that I do this. Thank you.

# Thank You

I deeply appreciate you spending the past couple of hundred pages with the characters and events of a world long past, yet hopefully relevant today.

If you enjoyed this book, I'd also be grateful for a kind review on your favorite bookseller's Web site or social media outlet. Word of mouth is the best way to make me successful, so that I can bring you even more high-quality stories of bygone times.

I'd love to hear directly from you, too—feel free to reach out to me via my Facebook page, Twitter feed, or Web site and let me know what you liked, and what you would like me to work on more.

Again, thank you for reading, for telling your friends about this book, for giving it as a gift or dropping off a copy in your favorite classroom or library. With your support and encouragement, we'll find even more times and places to explore together.

larsdhhedbor.com
Facebook: LarsDHHedbor
@LarsDHHedbor on Twitter

Enjoy a preview of the next book in the
*Tales From a Revolution* series:

# <u>**The Break**</u>

Susannah clutched the railing of the rickety-feeling ship as i plunged through what seemed to her the worst storm she' ever witnessed. She allowed as that she might not have tha much perspective on the nature of storms at sea; though she hac grown up in sight of the ocean, this was her first venture ont its broad—and at the moment, roiled—face.

She felt ill, and could not discern for certain whether i was the motion of the deck under her feet or the situation that hac placed her here that was the cause for the unsettled feeling in he belly.

Clamping her jaw shut, she peered out through th windswept mist, looking for and finding the sliver of shorelin visible along the horizon. It slid by just perceptibly, though i consisted entirely of undifferentiated forest, unbroken by an friendly seaside village or settlement.

Turning to look across the deck at the open ocean beyond she was glad to see no pinprick of white that might represent a unfriendly sail. Though her father had assured her that the rebel would not make so bold as to attack a merchant ship, she had com to distrust all assurances of stability and safety.

She could not grasp what, exactly, animated the rebels enmity toward the King, having only a dim awareness that affair between the Crown and Colonies had been edging toward disaster for almost as long as she could remember.

It seemed like only yesterday that she had crept out of her room one evening to hear her father and some of his friends discussing in urgent tones the latest outrages of the agitators against Parliament's acts.

A bottle of sack wine stood open upon the table, a lone remainder of a large and satisfying meal. A mostly-empty glass gripped tightly in his hand, a man named Mister Forrester, whom Susannah knew from her trips down to the docks with her father, was speaking, his face red with intensity.

"A perfectly reasonable levy, paying for the King's active and energetic defense of our shores from those French beasts, and they organize to refuse entry to any goods marked with the revenue stamp. What thin sort of gratitude is that, I ask you?"

"I cannot answer for their reasoning," Susannah's father replied. "Gratitude is not in them, I agree, but what's more, they have failed to avail themselves of the normal means of communication with the Crown, choosing instead to engage in riot and disorder to make their unhappiness known."

He shook his head, his face stony in resolve. "It is no wonder that His Majesty has felt the need to respond by sending additional customs agents here to restore us to the orderly practice of properly regulated and paid commerce that obtained before these malcontents began to raise a rabble."

Mister Hawlings, whose trade was not known to Susannah, spoke up now, his tone quiet and dangerous. "They are as small boys, playing with fire in a storehouse because it pleases them to see their shadows leap upon the walls. They will soon discover to their regret that they are not so large as their shadows permit them to believe that they are. Indeed, if they are not careful, they will set these Colonies ablaze, to the ruin of all around them."

Forrester seized upon this point, interjecting, "None will suffer so much as the proprietors of the storehouse—or society—that they so destroy."

His interlocutors nodded, their lips pursed and heads moving in such perfect synchrony that Susannah could not help but giggle at their matched expressions. Her father glanced up sharply in her direction, and she darted back into her room, her heart racing as she heard his step creaking across the floor behind her.

"You are to be abed and resting, not sneaking about eavesdropping on the private discussions of your elders." His face was no longer comical to behold, but stern and disapproving. She could see at the corners of his eyes, though, a hint of amusement, and she took assurance that she would be forgiven this transgression.

"Yes, Papa," she said quietly, pulling the old blanket that her mother had once used up to her chin and curling up under it meekly.

"I shall ask my friends to keep their voices down, so as not to further disturb your rest, then, and will expect not to see you again until the morning."

"Yes, Papa," she repeated.

Their voices had risen again as the wine in the bottle dropped further, but she had not again succumbed to the temptation to learn what animated their discussion, and could make out no more than small snatches of conversation as she drifted off.

Turning back to the distant shore now, though, she thought that she might have a better understanding of what they had been talking about.

There had come a terrifying afternoon when Forrester had appeared, wild-eyed, at their door, shouting to her father incoherently about tar and feathers, and Susannah grasped after too long that some terrible fate had befallen Hawlings.

The next time she saw the quiet, intense man who had sat at her father's table, he appeared to have been shorn of his hair, and moved stiffly, as though in substantial pain. His intense gaze held a new fire, and the girl was frightened enough to cross the street when she saw him from that time forward.

Too, she had heard talk around the town of a customs boat that had been set afire in an act that some feared would be taken as an act of open rebellion. A pole erected as a rallying point by the rioters was torn down by a group of men—including her father—who counted themselves as loyal to the Crown, despite being confronted with raised fists and angry words from the opponents of the customs service.

Not long after that, Susannah's slumber had been interrupted one night by a commotion outside the house. She heard her father's voice, angry and firm, answered by a jeering catcall. Something had thumped against the side of the house, followed by a sharp yelp from whoever was confronting the master of the house.

Her father had closed the door heavily behind him as he'd retuned inside, and she could hear him stirring restlessly in his bed throughout the remainder of that night. In the morning, though, he volunteered nothing about the incident, and deflected Susannah's questions brusquely.

The most recent confrontation had spurred her father to place them on this ridiculous little ship, pitching across the sea toward a destination as foreign to her as the mythical shores of the

Orient, though far closer.

Mister Graham, another of her father's friends had appeared at his step on a dreary morning, looking haggard and disheveled when she opened the door to greet him.

His voice full of weariness, he asked, "Is your father at home?"

"Yes, though he is engaged in his morning ablutions at the moment. Should you like to enter and wait for him?"

"I had better do so, as I know not whether I will be safe in open view."

Susannah frowned at this comment, but stood aside to grant him entry to the house. "I shall go and tell Papa that you await him," she said, a worried expression on her face.

She rushed to the back room of the house, where her father was nearly finished dressing himself for the day.

"Papa, Mister Graham has come to call on you, and waits in the kitchen. He looks very strange and out of sorts, as if something terrible has happened."

Her father looked sharply at her, saying, "You should finish preparing for your lessons with Miss Thayer. You may tell Mister Graham that I will greet him presently."

Susannah did as she was bidden, and though she dutifully tried to attend to the lessons in grammar and diction that Miss Thayer offered, her mind kept wandering back to Mister Graham, and she lost track of what her tutor was saying several times through the morning.

"Susannah, might you spare me your attention, or are you preoccupied by some event that I ought know of?"

"I am sorry, Miss Thayer," Susannah said solemnly. "I do

not know whether I am at liberty to speak of what is troubling me, but I will give you the fullest measure I can of my attention."

The usually kind-eyed tutor gave Susannah a stern look, but the girl's serious expression softened her heart. "Very well. Now, let us go over those declensions again..."

When Susannah returned home, she found her father in a state of high agitation.

"I fear that events have exceeded my ability to justify continuing to expose you to the risk of staying here in our comfortable home, Susannah," he said by way of greeting.

She gasped, "But then where will we go, Papa? Is there some neighbor with whom we must lodge? And what danger urges you to such a conclusion?"

"My compatriot, Mister Graham, lost his home to the action of a mob in the night. They gathered to riot without sometime after midnight, in an attempt to influence him to cease his efforts to defend the Crown from their violence and disorder. In a matter of less than an hour, they had raised themselves to such a fervor that they had fired his house and barn, and this stout servant of the King had no choice but to flee with but the clothing on his back."

His eyes haunted by a fear that Susannah had never before seen, he continued, "I will not stay here and expose you to the whims of the mob as they drag our community into the very flames of the hereafter."

"But, Papa, what of our friends and your business here? Will we leave them with so little notice?" She felt tears begin to form at the edges of her eyes as she thought about her close friend Emma, with whom she had shared confidences and play since before she could remember.

He regarded her seriously, answering, "I would rather that we leave swiftly and leave to Providence the security of our friendships and finances, and take no risk that I should awake one night to find I had failed your mother in her final charge upon me to keep you safe and happy."

He had been unmovable by any number of tears or words, and in a matter of days, they had packed what little they could, and they were crossing from the stability of the land that had cradled Susannah since her birth to the unsteady planks of the ship that now carried them away.

Look for **The Break: Tales From a Revolution - Nova-Scotia** at your favorite booksellers.

Made in United States
North Haven, CT
27 July 2024

55498239R00131